He felt as if he'd been punched in the gut.

His head felt as if it might fall off his shoulders, which seemed ludicrously appropriate considering that Rob would undoubtedly decapitate him if he seduced his good friend's daughter, his much-too-young daughter—even if she was fully grown and lush enough to tempt a man old enough to be her…much older brother.

Amber strolled down onto the aft deck, throwing out her arms and twirling in an expression of complete abandon. He gripped the wheel tightly, trained his gaze forward and began a desperate litany inside his head.

Too young. My friend's daughter. Too young. My friend's daughter. Too young. My friend's daughter.

An absolutely luscious woman.

He closed his eyes, deeply aware that he was in big trouble.

Dear Reader,

Although the anniversary is over, Silhouette Romance is still celebrating our coming of age—we'll soon be twenty-one! Be sure to join us each and every month for six emotional stories about the romantic journey from first time to forever.

And this month we've got a special Valentine's treat for you! Three stories deal with the special holiday for true lovers. Karen Rose Smith gives us a man who asks an old friend to *Be My Bride?* Teresa Southwick's latest title, *Secret Ingredient: Love,* brings back the delightful Marchetti family. And Carla Cassidy's *Just One Kiss* shows how a confirmed bachelor is brought to his knees by a special woman.

Amusing, emotional and oh-so-captivating Carolyn Zane is at it again! Her latest BRUBAKER BRIDES story, *Tex's Exasperating Heiress,* features a determined groom, a captivating heiress and the pig that brought them together. And popular author Arlene James tells of *The Mesmerizing Mr. Carlyle,* part of our AN OLDER MAN thematic miniseries. Readers will love the overwhelming attraction between this couple! Finally, *The Runaway Princess* marks Patricia Forsythe's debut in the Romance line. But Patricia is no stranger to love stories, having written many as Patricia Knoll!

Next month, look for appealing stories by Raye Morgan, Susan Meier, Valerie Parv and other exciting authors. And be sure to return in March for a new installment of the popular ROYALLY WED tales!

Happy reading!

Mary-Theresa Hussey

Mary-Theresa Hussey
Senior Editor

Please address questions and book requests to:
Silhouette Reader Service
U.S.: 3010 Walden Ave., P.O. Box 1325, Buffalo, NY 14269
Canadian: P.O. Box 609, Fort Erie, Ont. L2A 5X3

The Mesmerizing
Mr. Carlyle

ARLENE JAMES

SILHOUETTE *Romance*®

Published by Silhouette Books

America's Publisher of Contemporary Romance

To Crystal and Timothy,
who hopefully found their paradise in the Keys.
Much love, DAR

SILHOUETTE BOOKS

ISBN 0-373-19493-5

THE MESMERIZING MR. CARLYLE

Copyright © 2001 by Deborah A. Rather

This edition published by arrangement with Harlequin Books S.A.

Visit Silhouette at www.eHarlequin.com

Printed in U.S.A.

Books by Arlene James

Silhouette Romance

City Girl #141
No Easy Conquest #235
Two of a Kind #253
A Meeting of Hearts #327
An Obvious Virtue #384
Now or Never #404
Reason Enough #421
The Right Moves #446
Strange Bedfellows #471
The Private Garden #495
The Boy Next Door #518
Under a Desert Sky #559
A Delicate Balance #578
The Discerning Heart #614
Dream of a Lifetime #661
Finally Home #687
A Perfect Gentleman #705
Family Man #728
A Man of His Word #770
Tough Guy #806
Gold Digger #830
Palace City Prince #866
The Perfect Wedding #962
An Old-Fashioned Love #968
A Wife Worth Waiting For #974
Mail-Order Brood #1024
The Rogue Who Came To Stay #1061
Most Wanted Dad #1144
Desperately Seeking Daddy #1186
Falling for a Father of Four #1295
A Bride To Honor #1330
Mr. Right Next Door #1352
Glass Slipper Bride #1379
A Royal Masquerade #1432
In Want of a Wife #1466
The Mesmerizing Mr. Carlyle #1493

*This Side of Heaven

Silhouette Special Edition

A Rumor of Love #664
Husband in the Making #776
With Baby in Mind #869
Child of Her Heart #964
*The Knight, the Waitress
  and the Toddler* #1131
Every Cowgirl's Dream #1195
Marrying an Older Man #1235
Baby Boy Blessed #1285

Silhouette Books

Fortune's Children
Single with Children

The Fortunes of Texas
Corporate Daddy

ARLENE JAMES

grew up in Oklahoma and has lived all over the South. In 1976 she married "the most romantic man in the world." The author enjoys traveling with her husband, but writing has always been her chief pastime.

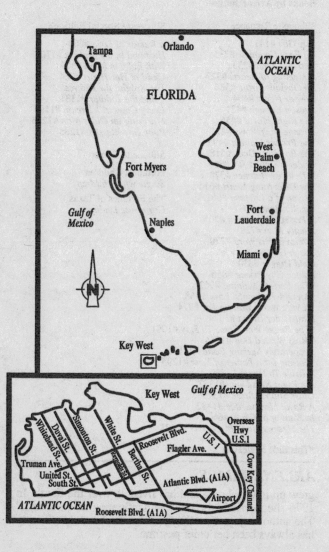

Chapter One

Amber Presley climbed the half-dozen steps to the tour office with rapid, purposeful strides, the wooden heels of her black, curled-toe shoes clacking sharply, brass buckles flashing from beneath the hem of her full black skirt, which she clutched in one hand. With the other, she checked the contents of her many pockets, including those of the voluminous black cape that currently threatened to choke her with its narrow ties. A single pat verified that each of the photographs, drawings and reproductions of old letters protected in clear plastic sleeves were in place, as well as a good-sized flashlight, small first aid kit and various minor pyrotechnic devices for effect. She hadn't had time to backcomb her long, dark red-brown hair, so she'd confined it in a black net snood and crammed the tall, pointed, broad-brimmed black hat on top of it. Heavy black eyeliner, bloodred lipstick, a black mole attached with adhesive and a long-sleeve black blouse completed the sweltering costume.

Even at ten o'clock at night, the Florida summer held

the temperature near ninety degrees. With the humidity hovering at ninety-five percent, Amber felt as though she was boiling inside her witchy costume. It was what she liked least about Key West, the incredible heat and humidity of this particular season. From the beginning of June to mid-September when the tradewinds finally arrived, not a breeze blew to lighten the triple-digit daytime heat or scatter the swarms of mosquitoes. The rest of the year the weather was moderate if somewhat boring, provided, of course, that the hurricane season was mild and the monsoon neither too long nor too wet. As a naive, twenty-one-year-old fresh out of college in the snowy northeast, she had not considered that she might grow tired of the tropical weather, that she might actually come to crave the turn of seasons, if not the vicious cold of northern winters, that the charms and romance of picturesque Key West might quickly pall for a girl interested in something more than the longest, on-going party in history. Three years had matured her in ways she had never imagined when she had impulsively decided to get as far away as possible from the winter cold and her overbearing parents.

She longed for Texas. Yes, the Dallas heat could bake your brain inside your skull in July and August if you were stupid enough to stand out under the sun bareheaded, but it wouldn't boil it while you sat in the shade fanning yourself. And after the summer, autumn actually came, complete with turning leaves and cool, crystalline days. Winter brought four or five weeks of truly cold weather, usually with at least one good ice storm, but then spring budded and blossomed and began its long buildup to summer misery. Unfortunately, Texas was also home to Robert and Happy Presley, her parents, who simply couldn't seem to accept the fact that their only child was entitled to live her own life as she saw fit.

Pushing through the heavy glass door at the top of the steps, Amber hurried into the small reception area and nodded to the balding, middle-age man behind the desk. "Hello, Conn. Sorry I'm late."

"Oh, it's only five or ten minutes," the agency owner replied offhandedly. All this time and Amber still had not adjusted to the laid-back attitude so common in the Keys. To her, time still meant something.

"My relief at the café was late," she explained, even as she picked up the tour list from the corner of the desk, "again."

The crowd was light for a Friday. Only about two dozen guests had signed up for Key West's most popular nighttime tour, a three-hour walking recitation of the city's most bizarre incidents, of which there were many, from murders and hangings to supposed hauntings and at least one lurid instance each of bigamy and obsession. All were matters of some historical documentation, but the tourists seemed to prefer to get even decades-old gossip person to person and on-site. Conducting the tour gave her a chance to actually employ her expensive thespian education, even if coincidentally, and earn a little extra cash, the latter being much more important to her than the former.

In truth, like the impulsive move to Key West, the decision to become an actress had been much more an exercise in sheer rebellion at her controlling father's method of parenting than a well-reasoned decision. Oh, she loved the theater, and in a very real sense, it had been her salvation. Theatrical people were so forgiving. In their world, one was allowed to be odd, socially backward, shy, uncertain, all of which she had been when she'd first arrived at the tony all-girls' college that her controlling, overprotective father had decided she must attend. Yes, the theater had given her much—except the desire to actually act. Nevertheless, every Friday and Saturday night she donned the witch's weeds and essentially told bedtime stories as if she actually believed them to adults and the occasional child for part-time wages and tips.

The extra cash came in handy. Every cent went into what she'd come to call her "escape fund." Her waitressing job barely paid the bills, for the cost of living in Key West was exorbitant. The second job was gradually making it possible for her to correct the mistake she'd made in moving here by relocating and finally beginning to build a life of which she could be justly proud—and maybe, just maybe, finally prove to her parents that she had truly grown up.

"Anything I should know?" she asked, scanning the list of unfamiliar names.

Conn shrugged. "I took two bottles of whiskey away from a group of six college students. I let them keep a bottle of beer apiece."

"Oh, Conn," Amber complained, "I thought we agreed the last time you saddled me with a bunch of drunks that this wouldn't happen again."

"I didn't say they were drunk, just feeling good."

Feeling good was the Key West euphemism for legally intoxicated but still standing. She hated drunks. She had truly come to despise the effects of overindulgence in alcohol. Perfectly nice people often became sick, nasty, sometimes even dangerous.

Sighing, she put out her hand. "Give me the phone."

Conn opened the middle drawer of the battered desk behind which he lounged and extracted the only cellular phone the company owned. He turned it on and placed it in her hand. It was simply a safety measure. In the event that a customer got out of hand or stepped off a curb and twisted an ankle, she could call for assistance. She slipped the phone into the pocket of her voluminous skirt and walked out the back door into the alley, where her group waited in semidarkness. The light over the narrow back stoop provided the perfect spot for a small, outlandishly costumed woman to make a suitable entrance, and she did so with flourish, furling her cape with one hand.

"Good evening, my ladies and gents. Welcome to the dark side of Key West. I am your tour guide, Amber Rose, and it is my privilege and pleasure to bewitch you this night with eccentricity, murder and ghosts. A little business and we'll be on our way." As she spoke, she surveyed the gathered crowd.

Most of the group comprised couples wearing the usual shorts, T-shirts and athletic shoes. The drinkers were definitely college-age, four young men in muscle shirts and two twittering girls in suggestive clothing. Only one individual stood out among them, a thirtyish man in safari shorts, top-siders and a khaki shirt with the sleeves rolled back over strong, deeply tanned forearms. Obviously alone, he stood apart from the others, hands in his pockets, sun-streaked hair a little long and windblown. She knew the type, a sailor, a wealthy one, no doubt, with a yacht of his own and money enough to enjoy it. Key West saw many of the sort, but they usually had a scantily clad blonde hanging on one arm. Few of them ever attended her tour.

She went on smoothly. "I know my colleague, Mr. Snow, has counted your coins, collected your signed releases and made you aware of the rules of participation, so I will only say, at this point, that I strongly advise you each to make use of the restrooms conveniently located at either end of the building here, especially those of you who have recently imbibed. There are no restrooms for our use along the tour, and urinating in public is not only unsanitary but illegal. And it disturbs the ghosts." After a dramatic pause, she finished with, "In ten minutes time, I shall introduce you to them." With that, she slipped a small paper ball from one of her many pockets, tossed it to the ground below, setting off a tiny explosion of light and smoke, and stepped quickly backward through the already open door, leaving laughter and a smattering of applause behind her.

Precisely ten minutes later, she reappeared, at the end of the alley this time, the flashlight, hidden in the folds of her cape and pointing upward from beneath her chin, making her round, high-cheeked face appear as broad and flat as a full moon with garish red lips and long, wide cat eyes of gold. With a swirl of her cape, she turned and signaled her company to follow. They gathered quickly at her back and set off.

She began her spiel with an overview of the island's history. From a haven for shipwreckers who depended upon an outlying coral reef to provide the booty to an incubator for artists, writers, musicians and eccentrics, the Keys had flavored the American experience with tropical hedonism, taking less seriously its situation as southernmost outpost of republican freedom and embracing enthusiastically the natural freedoms found in sun, sand, water and relative isolation. Due to that isolation, the so-called "Conch Republic" was a near fact, an ephemeral and cerebral nation empowered by fabulous sunsets, individuality and the right, generously given and reciprocated, to party down. Said republic had afforded place and longevity to some of the strangest free and/or tortured spirits recorded in the minor annals of coincidental history, among them a mortician who stole and set up housekeeping with the corpse of his beloved, an evil doll animated by voodoo and a minister who burned to death his unfaithful wife and her Sunday school class of innocent children. At each stop along the way, Amber pointed out the architectural significance of the surrounding historical edifices and gave interesting anecdotal asides before delivering the mysterious, creepy or downright odd vignettes for which the tour—and the city—were famed.

Once, as expected, the tour was heckled by a group of local teenagers cruising the streets of Old Town. Amber had learned early on that neither admonishment nor lack of attention would placate these bored mischief-makers; so she had incorporated their pranks into the presentation, delivering as needed comical curses and ludicrous spells that elicited laughter and applause from her groups, seemed to satisfy the pranksters or put them in their place and left control firmly in her own small hands. Some of the area residents were so amused by her antics that a symbiotic sort of relationship had arisen wherein various individuals literally lay in wait on certain nights in order to heckle and tease, giving her an opportunity to play out, as it were, her particular bag of tricks. These were now old, if casual, friends, and she shamelessly employed them to keep herself from growing bored with and stale in her presentation.

Due to its reduced numbers, the tour went quickly and smoothly that night. She experienced no problems and was able to devote more time than usual to questions from the gallery. Surprisingly, the college group appeared literally spellbound, no doubt as much owing to the alcohol they'd imbibed than any expertise on her part. Through it all, the lone gentleman with the virile seafarer's looks remained aloof, smiling benignly and sometimes cryptically at her performance. Of all the group, she'd have said that he was least interested in the stories she had to tell. She was, therefore, surprised when he patiently waited for the group to disperse then approached her personally.

"Well done," he said, bestowing upon her a genuine smile that fairly dazzled. "I had my doubts, frankly, but I must admit to having been thoroughly entertained."

He truly was a handsome character of no more than medium height and build with a tanned, squarish face having a strong jawline and chin, a slightly jutting brow over light, hazel green eyes decorated at the outer edges with tiny crow's-feet and a straight but not-too-prominent nose over a spare, perfectly shaped mouth. With all that sun-streaked, wind-ruffled, salt spray-roughened hair flowing back from a broad forehead, he could easily have played the part of pirate. What he was doing in her tour group on a Friday night remained a mystery, one she was not inclined to solve.

Keeping in character, Amber inclined her head regally. "I thank you, and the spirits thank you."

He chuckled at that, seeming oddly pleased. "You're welcome, all of you."

Considering the conversation closed, Amber started off down the alley toward the back door atop the stoop of the tour office. The man quickly stepped abreast of her, keeping pace easily.

"Uh, listen, my name is Reece Carlyle, and I'm new to the island. Just arrived yesterday afternoon, actually. And I was wondering, since you're a tour guide and all, if you could give me some pointers."

Ah. One of those. She was used to encountering men on the prowl more often in the restaurant where she regularly worked than on the tour, but she was adept at handling these attempted pickups. "Certainly." As she spoke, she slowly climbed the steps of the back stoop. "Watch your wallet. Stay in the light. Expect to pay top dollar in Old Town and be unappreciated elsewhere. Get used to walking. Drink plenty of fluids." She stopped on the landing and leaned slightly over the handrail. "And be sure to see the maritime museum. Some of the artifacts discovered by treasure hunters off this coast are fascinating." Turning away, she fit her key into the lock on the back door and turned it. "Oh, and do employ the two most important tools of survival in the Keys, sunscreen and mosquito repellant," she added, pulling open the door. Then, turning a smile over one shoulder, she walked into the building. "Good night, Mr. Carlyle." The door closed smoothly at her back. Setting the lock, she immediately began stripping away her heavy, damp costume, beginning with the mole. At least the flirts were getting better-looking, she mused idly.

Conn had already left the building, though technically he was supposed to stay at the desk near the telephone until the tour ended. Amber was resigned to, if not approving of, this behavior. The average Conch, as the native Key Westians liked to call themselves, was so laid back and tolerant that he could barely conceive of intentional evil-doing and trusted with childlike innocence in the benevolent randomness of accidents. Amber, however, despite the heavy-handed overprotectiveness of her paternal parent, possessed a much more refined sense of responsibility and a far keener sense of possibility. That being the case, she had programmed the emergency police and medical number into the first position on the speed dial of the company cell phone, which she now returned to the desk drawer.

After bundling her costume and props into the convenient folds of her cape, she stepped into the sandals she had extracted from one of those voluminous pockets, coiled her long, thick hair atop her head and secured it with a clip. Then she locked up the office, hoisted her cumbersome packet and began the long walk home. Morning came early for those who didn't regularly drink themselves insensible and worked actual jobs.

Despite what he was sure was good advice, Reece stood in the shadow of a huge magnolia and watched, bemused, as the daughter of one of his best friends and erstwhile business associates set off at a clip down the sidewalk, a big black bundle slung over one shoulder. Amber Rose Presley was petite to the point of diminutive, her girlish face a picture of true innocence beneath the garish cosmetics. In costume she looked like a pretty gnome. The shorts and T-shirt exposed her as the lovely child she was. No wonder Robert was so worried about her that he'd asked Reece to look her up and check out her situation—strictly confidentially, of course.

Robert had been able to keep track of her in a general way. He had ascertained fairly easily where she worked and received her mail, but as she refused all correspondence from him and her mother, was of legal age and had landed herself in the one small town in America where the local authorities literally laughed at Rob's concerns, there was little else he could do. When Reece had announced his plans, more than a year after his separation and divorce, to sail around the coast of the Gulf of Mexico port to port, Robert had pleaded with him to stop in Key West and check up on his little Amber Rose.

Little was the operative word. The girl couldn't have stood five feet tall. His own eleven-year-old daughter, Brittany, was four-feet-eight already and showed every sign of being as tall as her mother one day. He'd say this much for Amber, however, she'd handled that silly tour with all the aplomb and finesse of the trained actress she was, and she'd wielded quite a firm hand, as well. He'd fully expected trouble from those beer-swigging kids, and when that carload of teenagers had cruised slowly by hurling insults, he'd been ready to come to the rescue, but she'd managed all with ease. When one of the beer drinkers had casually tossed aside his empty, Amber had instructed him coolly to retrieve it. Litter, like urinating in public, offended the spirits—and their guide. He hoped, trusted, that Brit would one day understand and enjoy her own personal power so well. He prayed, however, that she would never be so hardheaded and rebellious as to cut herself off from those who loved her most.

Brittany had her own problems just now, poor kid. Even after a year, she had not become reconciled to the divorce. Perhaps, Reece mused, as her parents they had protected her too much from the unhappiness with which they had each struggled over the years. The divorce had been a very long time coming, and he had wanted it no less than Joyce. Nevertheless, for Brit's sake alone, he'd have stuck it out for at least a few more years, had not Joyce decided that she was getting no younger and wanted the chance to start over.

At thirty-eight and one year her senior, Reece had seen her point. He was feeling well worn and badly used himself. Businesswise, he figured he had lots of good years left in him; romantically, he'd had to accept the fact that he was pretty much over the hill. Joyce, however, was an attractive woman, and she had moved almost immediately into a relationship with a longtime associate of his, one Mike Allen, three years divorced, the father of two boys. Some of Reece's friends wondered, due to the suddenness and intensity of the situation, if the relationship might not have started rather too soon—before the divorce, actually. Reece had thought about it and realized that he really didn't care one way or another, which in itself was as pathetic an assessment of his failed marriage as anything could be. Brittany was having a little trouble accepting a new man in her mother's life, however, especially since they had announced their intention to marry. Reece trusted that she would come around once she saw her mother truly happy. He hoped so, anyway. He truly bore Joyce no ill will.

The divorce was not without cost, of course. Not only was his little girl disappointed and confused, but a family bond of almost fourteen years had been sundered. Half of his daughter's grandparents were no longer his in-laws, her aunts and uncles no longer his sisters and brothers by marriage, and of course the same held true for his ex-wife. And then the business had come into play.

Reece had worked hard to make Carlyle Systems a success, perhaps harder than he might have if he'd been happy at home. The divorce had forced the sale of the company, the result being significant financial security for his daughter, his ex and himself. It had also essentially gutted his life. Except for his daughter, he found himself at loose ends. He could consult, of course. He still knew more about integrated business computer systems than ninety-nine percent of the world, and that expertise had already been tapped by several business groups in Houston, his base of operations. But consulting seemed to lack something important just now. Everything seemed to lack something important just now, which was exactly why he was standing here on a sidewalk in Key West, Florida.

Having grown up in Corpus Christi and lived many years in Houston, availing himself of the pleasures to be found on the Texas coast of the Gulf of Mexico, Reece had a natural affinity for the water. So, when he'd decided to take some time to get his head straight and figure out what to do with the rest of his life, six months on his boat, the *Merry Haven*, had seemed the perfect way to do it. Making his easy way around the Gulf, port by port, had taken three lazy months, and he could now say two things with confidence. One, simple contentment was grossly underrated. He'd found a large measure of it out on the blue water alone. It wasn't the delirious, ecstatic sort of glee that people seemed to chase so desperately, but it was very real. Except for missing his daughter, with whom he took great pains to stay in touch, he was principally happy in a way that he hadn't suspected he could be. Two, his own company was not as difficult to take as he'd feared. The long, miserable years of his marriage, the unmistakable truth that his wife had ceased early on to love him, had formed in him the notion that he was somehow to blame, somehow lacking. He no longer believed that.

He had searched his heart and come to the conclusion that he had done the best he could in a bad situation. Yes, he took responsibility for the choices he'd made. At twenty-four, with the first whiff of success in his nostrils, he had believed himself infallible, which accounted for the fact that he'd made a poor choice in marrying the only woman in his life at the time. Reece Carlyle, he freely admitted, was a one-woman man. He'd dated a good deal, but he'd always concentrated on one girlfriend at a time. Suddenly, he'd found that he could support a wife, so it had simply been time to have one, and Joyce had been the one girl in his orbit at that particular moment. By the time Brittany had been born only three years later, he'd known he'd made a mistake. He suspected Joyce had known it as well. But they had made a child together, and nothing and no one was more important to either of them than her. The situation had quickly deteriorated to the point, however, where they'd mutually agreed that having more children would be irresponsible and untenable.

So now here he stood, alone on a sidewalk in the dark in Key West, Florida, wondering what Amber Rose Presley would think if she knew that he had not been trying to pick her up earlier, only hoping to find out how she was getting on as a favor to her father. He'd been warned that honesty would not be the best policy where Miss Amber Rose was concerned. Any indication that Rob was behind this "chance meeting" would very likely have Amber fleeing into the night even faster than his own clumsy attempt at conversation. The problem now was how to find out what he needed to know. Surely it wasn't enough just to report that she was alive, apparently healthy and a better than average guide of goofy tours. If she were *his* daughter, he would certainly want to know more than that.

Sliding his hands into his pockets, Reece turned down the quiet, dark street and headed back toward the boardwalk dock and the rented skiff that would return him to the spot where the *Merry Haven* rested at anchor on the outer edge of Conch Harbor. All the slips at the city marina were currently filled, so he was stuck in the noisy, busy harbor. It made getting back and forth to the wharf difficult, but he could manage. Disappointed that he hadn't been able to engage Amber in meaningful conversation, he headed back to the boat for a late dinner of whatever he had left in the galley and sleep.

Along the way he passed graceful, picturesque old buildings—and homeless persons huddling in doorways and on porches. It was early yet by Key West standards, or so the college kids on the tour had told him, but as he drew near Eaton Street, the increase in traffic was pronounced. Much of it was foot traffic, but the street was clogged with taxis, private automobiles and pedicabs, tricycles with a bench seat for passengers between the two back wheels. Everyone was headed for Duval Street, which Amber had described for the tour as offering more alcohol per square foot than any piece of real estate in the United States. Personally, he doubted that it could compete with Bourbon Street in New Orleans, but he was willing to concede that it was not where he wanted to be tonight.

Tomorrow, he would call Brit again to make plans for picking her up for the final month of her summer vacation. Then he'd buy a few groceries and take in a little more of the town. Sunday was up for grabs. On Monday he'd take himself to an early dinner at a café on west Angela Street, where he had it on good authority that a certain someone worked first shift. With luck, he'd be able to talk to her again, find out what her current situation was and perhaps even discover what her plans for the future might be. Maybe, if he was very, very careful and a lot smarter than he had been tonight, he could even encourage her to go back home to her parents in Dallas.

That was probably a lot to ask of a single meeting at her workplace, however. Better plan on just winning enough of her confidence to get her to meet privately with him, but how was he to do that without making her think he was hitting on her? If he wasn't careful, he was going to come off like a lecherous older man out to seduce a naive younger woman, and the very idea disturbed him. He despised such men. He equally hated the duplicity he was forced to perform, too, but ultimately he was doing this for her own good, and that had to count for something.

Surely he could convince the girl to sit down someplace safe but quiet and tell him about herself. To his surprise, he found that he was actually looking forward to it. Amber Rose Presley was young, and according to some evidence and her own father, foolish, but she was also quite engaging. Or perhaps he had been too long alone with his own company. Either way, Miss Amber had not seen the last of him, though little did she know it.

He began to plan what he might say and do to draw her out and win her confidence. He'd always been good at client presentations, after all. Why should this be any different than winning a new account? He might not have a lot of romantic charm left, but he still had some business savvy upon which to call. And he was more mature than her, much more mature. Surely he could manage this. He had a good deal of experience managing headstrong little girls, after all. Yes, that was the ticket.

Amber was just another Brittany, several years older, perhaps, but essentially still a child. He would handle her as he would one of Brit's bouncy friends. A little charm, a little indulgence, a little authority and superiority. Friendly but somewhat aloof. Confident that he had a handle on the situation now, he took himself off to the safe haven of his boat, content with his personal delusions.

Chapter Two

"I need a full of half shells, a fritter ap and a burger, medium, hold the red, table six."

Amber slapped the ticket onto the shoulder-high counter and moved to the drinks station. Working quickly, she filled one small and two large glasses with ice, set them beneath the proper spigots and hit the proper buttons, filling them with three different varieties of bubbling soda. Grabbing a small round tray, she placed the glasses on it, hefted it atop her upturned palm and swept around the partition into the small dining room, avoiding an incoming busboy as she did so. Ten seconds later, she placed the filled glasses on the table, dispensed smiles and moved on to take the next order, tucking the tray under her arm as she withdrew a pair of thin cork coasters from her apron pocket.

She saw as soon as she drew alongside the booth that she had in hand one coaster too many. Dropping the extra back into her pocket, she slid the other onto the plank tabletop, extracted her order pad and plucked her pen from her ponytail. "Hi, welcome to…"

The seafarer smiled back at her. His thick, windblown hair had been tamed into a semblance of order. Brushed away from the hairline, it waved across the back of his head and curled raggedly about his collar. Those light, mottled green eyes crinkled at the edges with his smile. He was even more attractive in the daytime than the evening.

"Hello," he said. "You're looking a little different today."

She searched her mind for his name and found it, part of it, anyway. "Reece, ah…" She snapped her fingers in an effort to jog her memory and finally came up with, "Carter?"

"Carlyle."

"Oh, yeah. Carlyle." She clicked the point down on her pen and scribbled the number of his table on the corner of the ticket, wondering if she should be worried. He had approached her after the tour with a lame come-on, and now here he sat at one of her tables. The next moment, she dismissed the notion. No man this good-looking had to dog a woman. Key West was a small island, only two by four miles. Old Town was much smaller. Naturally they were going to run into each other. "What can I get you, Mr. Carlyle?"

"Reece, please."

She shrugged. "Okay. Reece. Now, can I get you a drink while you look at the menu?"

"I think I need a little help first," he said, glancing over the menu. He sighed and looked up again. "What would you recommend, Amber?"

His use of her given name struck her as oddly familiar, but she couldn't imagine why. "What are you in the mood for? On the seafood side, our conch fritters are very popular. The chowder's my personal favorite, but if you ask me, it's too warm for it this time of year. Seafood aside, our burgers are fine, and the steaks are excellent, if a tad pricey. The Caribbean chicken breast is especially good, too, if you like mango and that sort of thing.''

"I like mango and that sort of thing,'' he said decisively, closing the menu. "Caribbean chicken it is.''

She wrote that down, asking, "Onion rings, fries or baked potato with that?''

"Baked potato, I think, with everything.''

"That's a b-pot loaded. Salad dressing?''

"Honey mustard, I think.''

"Works for me. What to drink?''

"Iced tea.''

"Orange, lime, raspberry or regular?''

He chuckled at that. "Regular will do fine.''

"I'll have it out in a jif.''

She reached for the menu. He snatched it up and handed it to her, saying, "I, um, like this costume better than the other, by the way.'' She glanced down at the baggy khaki shorts and androgynous green knit polo which, along with running shoes, white socks and green mini apron, comprised her work uniform.

"Gee, thanks. That puts you in a minority of one on this island. Around here, the general rule of thumb is the wilder the better.''

"You don't strike me as the wild type.''

"No, but I am the witchy type,'' she told him, clicking down the tip of her pen and stabbing it into her ponytail again. "I'd better turn this in before the dinner rush hits.'' She waved the order check and moved away.

Definitely on the make, this guy. Maybe she ought to recommend a bar to him, one where the college crowd didn't congregate. Or maybe he liked them young, and that was why he was picking on her. She'd have to let him know, if it came handy, that she was older than she looked. Maybe that would put him off. It was a pity, really. The man was truly fine. He was also a tourist, a passer-through, and even if he weren't, she had no business getting involved with him or anyone, since she, too, was on her way off the island, eventually. Meanwhile, she had work to do.

She turned in the order, dropped off his iced tea and went about her business. When his order came up, she delivered it with as little fanfare and conversation as possible. Per her personal policy, she checked on him once, according to the number of persons in his party, then returned to take away the empties and offer him dessert.

"I think I can just squeeze in a piece of Key lime pie," he decided.

"Good choice," she commented, writing the order down.

"Where would I find a Key lime grove, by the way?" he asked conversationally.

"India," she replied wryly. "There are none in the Florida Keys."

"Well, that's a kick."

"Isn't it? I'll have that pie out in a minute."

"Take your time."

But time was something she never seemed to have much of, especially on weekends. She had another tour to conduct tonight, and she had little doubt that it would make last night's tame venture look like child's play. With that thought in mind, she disposed of the empties and fetched the pie, leaving the check with it at his table. "I'll get that whenever you're ready."

Without waiting for a reply, she spun off and moved on. A quarter-hour later, she returned to pick up the payment, a fifty for a sixteen dollar tab. "Be right back with your change."

He smiled and sat back as if settling in for a lengthy wait. She turned in an order and saw the cashier, who rang up the purchase, filed the tab and counted out the change,

thirty-three bucks and coins. When she dropped it off, he
snagged her by the wrist to keep her from hurrying on.
"I'm sorry," he apologized, immediately releasing her. "I,
um…" He laughed uncomfortably. "I'm not very good at
this. I thought it would be simple, but, um, it's not turning
out that way."

She folded her arms. The approach was unique at least,
but she really didn't have the time to devote to playing it
out. "Look, I'm working here."

"Yes, I realize that. It's part of the problem actually."
He looked at her hopefully. "If we could just talk for a
few minutes?"

Oh, boy, here we go, she thought. She huffed a big sigh,
letting him know she'd covered this ground before. "Mr.
Carlyle—"

"Reece."

"Mr. Carlyle," she repeated firmly, "I'm flattered,
but—"

"I just want to talk, honestly."

She went on as if he hadn't interrupted her. "I am *not*
interested."

"In a little conversation?" he asked.

"In anything. Conversation, friendship, flirtation, one-
night stands, affairs. Anything. Got it?"

"If you would just sit down with me for a little while,
we could…get to know one another."

She pressed the tip of her forefinger between her brows
and closed her eyes. "What part of 'no' do you not understand?"

"Please."

Amazingly, she almost cratered. What could a few
minutes hurt? Then she realized what she was doing and
stiffened her spine. "I have customers waiting, Mr. Carlyle. You have a nice day." She started off, and he came
to the very edge of his seat.

"Amber, wait."

She stopped, passed a look over her shoulder and brought a hand to one hip. "Or," she said flatly, "I can have you tossed. Your choice." It was a bald-faced bluff. The management was about as likely to toss a sober customer as they were to throw money in the aisles.

Reece Carlyle flattened his mouth, pinched the bridge of his nose and nodded.

She walked away without another word. Funny, but she felt downright depressed all of a sudden. She shook it off, hurrying back to work with determined energy. A little while later, she cast a surreptitious look at the booth and found it empty, except for a number of bills presumably left as a tip. Something that felt very like disappointment hit her. Silly that, foolish in the extreme, and she'd had enough of foolishness. She'd promised herself over two years ago that she was going to be sensible, and she'd been good to her word ever since. She would remain so now. Even if it killed her.

Reece mentally kicked himself a dozen times before he got out the café door to the sidewalk. What was wrong with him? Why couldn't he find his ground with this girl? He felt like a stuttering schoolboy when he tried to talk to her, and he couldn't think of a reason for it—except one. It had to be the lie. He didn't know how to deal in half-truths and omissions. The task itself was honorable. Her parents were concerned for her welfare. He happened to be in the neighborhood and looked her up in hopes of reassuring them and possibly being of service to her. What was wrong with that? No, it wasn't what he was doing, it was the way he was doing it.

He came to a conclusion. Robert Presley's assertions and advice aside, he was going to have to tell her the truth. Surely she would talk to him for a few minutes then, even if it was to rail against her parents' interference in her life, though this couldn't really be called interference, just curiosity, concern. She wouldn't be unreasonable enough to refuse him a few minutes of her time then, surely. Taken in one light, her treatment of him and his approach was quite sensible for a single young woman in these surroundings. Obviously she'd had experience fending off advances, and she was quite firm about it. Her father ought to be pleased about that, at least.

With his decision made, he felt somewhat better about his situation. Now all he had to do was find out what time she got off work, wait around for a chance to speak to her, confess all and hope for the best. Ascertaining what time the shift ended required only a return to the café, a moment and a single question of the cashier. Only when he found himself once more on the sidewalk and spotted a van parked in the alleyway and a delivery man carrying a box around the back of the building did Reece wonder if she might leave the café by a different route than the front. He rubbed the back of his neck with one hand thoughtfully, decided a little reconnoitering was in order, and ambled as casually as he could manage around the building where he, indeed, found two doors, one marked for deliveries, the other for employees only.

With that bit of information in mind, he took himself off to explore idly for a couple hours, marveling at the shops and the advertised prices for goods. He'd been appalled at the cost of groceries earlier. He was no less appalled now at the price asked for clothing, shoes and what might be politely called souvenirs. The only thing reasonably priced in Key West seemed to be alcoholic beverages. That impression was reinforced when he picked up a real estate brochure and spent some time poring over the listings, which included modest three-bedroom houses for half a million bucks and used, single-bedroom mobile homes on canals for over a hundred thousand. He could imagine what rent was like. No wonder Amber worked two jobs. He was surprised anyone but the very rich could survive here for long.

He considered returning to the boat, because it was definitely cooler out on the water, but it was a long walk back to the wharf in this heat. It was too late to visit any of the museums or other points of interest for the day. He wished he'd thought to bring with him the novel he was currently reading, but he honestly hadn't imagined that things would turn out this way.

Rather naively, he'd imagined that he would make polite overtures and she would respond with conversation, which would lead to a casual invitation to continue talking at a more convenient time. He'd never expected to find it so difficult to engage her. He winced when he thought about some of the inane openings he'd tried.

I like this costume better.

Where would I find a Key lime grove, by the way?

He hadn't been so inept since high school.

Eventually it was time to take up his predetermined position at the corner of the building. By so doing, he could keep an eye on each door. He waited another quarter-hour before a taxi pulled up into the alleyway and came to a stop just beyond where he waited. The driver, a tall, lanky fellow with a mousy brown ponytail and a scraggly goatee, killed the engine and got out to lounge against the fender. Reece nodded at the man and looked away. Several minutes later, Reece checked his watch and from the corner of his eye caught the other guy doing the same. They shared a smile over that—and continued to wait.

Finally, the sound of a slamming screen door alerted them both. The taxi driver straightened away from the car and looked expectantly toward the back of the building. Reece became aware of a knot forming in his stomach even before Amber came around the corner and hurried toward the taxi driver, saying, ''I'm sorry I'm late, Walt. Carrie still hasn't showed up, but I told the boss I couldn't stay any longer. Do we have time to run by the tour office before we go home?'' As she spoke, the driver rushed around the car and opened the front passenger door for her.

''Sure, babe, whatever you need,'' he said, literally handing her into the seat. She glanced pointedly at Reece as ''Walt'' hurried back to his side of the car, then just as pointedly she looked away, clearly dismissing him.

Babe...before we go home.

The knot in Reece's stomach tightened and expanded. Good grief, why hadn't he thought of this? She had a boyfriend, a live-in boyfriend, apparently! At first he was dismayed; then suddenly he was angry. He stood with his hands on his hips and watched the taxi back up and drive away with Amber inside. He couldn't believe he hadn't thought of this. Worse, he couldn't believe that she was with *that* guy! He was too tall for her, too scraggly, too...not right. Oh, boy, was Rob ever going to explode when he heard this!

Disappointed, disgusted and he wasn't sure what else, Reece had no choice but to head back toward his boat. And to think he'd cooled his heels all this time hoping just to speak to the girl! He started off at a clip, but the heat soon caught up with him, slowing him appreciably. When the anger wore off, he stopped to take stock of the situation and bleakly concluded that he had just two options. One, he could sail away from this place with what he knew now, or, two, he could hang around a little while longer and try again later, with the truth this time and perhaps a bit of a lecture. He was still dazed by the strength of his reaction— and the complete unsuitability of that guy! What was she thinking?

On the other hand, he wasn't sure he even wanted to know. Suddenly he knew what he had to do, what he had to try to do. If she were his daughter, it was what he would want from a friend. Somehow he had to get her off this island and away from that…that *taxi driver*. How the devil he was supposed to do it, though, was currently beyond him.

Amber bit her lip and looked out the window of the cab, wondering what she should do. The seafarer had obviously been waiting for her, and she was partly thrilled and partly alarmed. One heard such lurid tales of stalkers these days. And yet he seemed like such a nice man, well mannered, cultured, even, and yet oddly diffident, as if he didn't quite know how to approach her. He seemed frankly harmless and yet wildly virile. And he made her uncomfortable in a way she couldn't quite identify. Perhaps she should have spoken to him. On the other hand, what would be the point? She just didn't know what to think.

"Did you see that guy back there?" she asked Walt. He slid her a questioning look.

"The one standing at the corner of the building? Yeah, sure. Why?"

"He was in my tour last Friday night, and afterward he, um, well, he tried to talk to me."

Walt sat up a little straighter. "Yeah? About what?"

"Oh, nothing, really." She shrugged. "I gave him the brush-off, and that was that. I thought."

"Meaning?"

"He showed up at the restaurant today, about three hours ago, I guess, and it was the same thing, except he was more persistent."

Walt sat forward suddenly, hunching over the steering wheel. "Persistent how?"

"He said he wanted to get to know me, to talk."

Walt frowned, his thin brows drawing together over his hawkish nose. "You didn't talk to him, did you?"

"You know I don't have time for that sort of thing, certainly not when I'm working."

"You didn't make a date for later?"

"No! Of course not." But she'd wanted to. She looked away.

"You think he was waiting for you?"

"I don't know. I told him that I wasn't interested, but...I don't know what to think."

"You want me to take care of this?" Walt demanded. "What's his name? Any idea where he's staying?"

"No! No." She realized suddenly what it was she really wanted to know, and it surprised her. She cleared her throat, trying to get comfortable with the idea, and unconsciously smoothed her hair. "You, um, you think a guy like that might actually be interested in me?" she asked her old friend and roommate.

Walt gaped at her. "You kidding me? You just give him half a chance and see if he don't jump all over you."

Amber brightened automatically. "Really? You think?" Not that she'd give him the chance, of course.

Walt's gaze turned worried. "Listen, Amber, this guy could be a stalker or something—a mass murderer, even."

She laughed, dismissing the notion out of hand. "Oh, no. He's not the type. Actually, he's kind of sweet."

"There is no 'type,'" Walt argued. "Maybe you better let me talk to him."

She waved a hand. "Ah, I'll probably never see him again. You know how it is around here. People breeze in, and they breeze out again."

"Not everybody," Walt pointed out. "You didn't."

"Wish I had," she muttered.

"Aw, you don't mean that," he said. "Yeah, it's expensive and sometimes it's inconvenient, but, hey, that's the price you pay for living in paradise.''

"Paradise?" Amber echoed skeptically, shaking her head. "You know, I bought into that whole paradise thing when I first came here. Then about three weeks later I realized I was stuck on this tiny island without a penny to my name surrounded by a bunch of eternal adolescents who wouldn't know paradise if they tripped over it."

"It's not that bad," Walt argued. "Sure, there's a party atmosphere, but it's gotta have something going for it or else all these wealthy part-timers wouldn't be hanging around running up the price of everything."

"Okay, maybe for the wealthy it's a kind of paradise," she conceded ungraciously, "but not for the rest of us."

"I like it here," Walt said. "It's laid-back and easy. Nobody judges anybody else. I mean, it's expensive, but I can get by, and the heat don't bother me, much, not when it's so nice the rest of the year. I just don't see what's not to like."

Amber sighed. They'd had this conversation before. "I guess I just want more—more opportunity, more culture, more variety. I want a chance to do something with my life, Walt. Is that so hard to understand?"

"Why can't you have that here?" Walt asked, spreading his big hands over the steering wheel.

Amber just stared at him. Walt would never understand. He'd come here to the island from Alabama almost ten years ago and was perfectly happy sharing an apartment with three other people and "getting by," so long as no one hassled or hurried him. He was a simple man, Walt, and a good friend, but he just didn't get her at all. He would never understand that the very things about the island which he found so satisfying were what she found completely stultifying. "Never mind," she said. "It doesn't matter."

He nodded and plucked at his goatee. For a moment they rode in silence. Then suddenly he said, "You don't ever have any fun. Why don't we go out tonight?"

Amber stared at him. "But we both have to work."

"Ditch it."

She shook her head. It was so Walt, so Key West, that attitude. A good time should always take precedence. "I can't."

"Why not?"

"I want to work."

"You work too much," he grumbled.

She sighed inwardly. She was talking to someone from another culture. He just didn't, couldn't, get it. "I need the money," she said softly.

He rolled his eyes but said nothing more on the subject. Instead, he asked, "What about that guy?"

"What about him?"

"I still think maybe I ought to talk to him, tell him to stay away from you."

"No need for that," she told him lightly. "I very much doubt I'll see him again. He'll be long gone soon." She felt certain of that. Yes, Reece Carlyle would soon disappear from the island if he hadn't already. And so would she, hopefully. But not soon enough. Not soon enough.

Amber trudged up the open stairway, her bundled costume tossed over one shoulder as usual. She was tired and bored and somewhat depressed, though she really couldn't say why. The tour group had actually been more tame than she'd expected, and the night was a little cooler than normal. Add to that the fact that tomorrow was Sunday and her one true day off, and she should have felt happy, not glum. Nevertheless, she'd refused Walt's repeated offer of a night on the town. She hadn't even wanted to accept a ride home from him tonight. She only knew that she was in no mood for company.

Reaching the landing, she tried the door and found it open. Obviously at least one of her three roommates was at home—or Sharon had gone out and left the apartment door unlocked again. Though at twenty-six she was older than Amber by two years, Sharon displayed a remarkable propensity for irresponsibility. The woman blew off her bartending job at will, partied away her money, paid her bills late if at all and frequently had "overnight guests" even though the others in the apartment repeatedly asked her not to. They'd have gotten rid of her long ago if her name wasn't on the lease with Amber's and Walt's. Linda, the fourth roomie, had come along later. Linda was only twenty-one and not only worked waiting tables at the same café as Amber but also shared one of the three bedrooms with her. Amber worried about her. The girl was young and impressionable and still deciding how she was going to live her life. In many ways, she reminded Amber of herself not so long ago. Lately, Sharon seemed to take a perverse pleasure in shocking the girl.

Amber shoved the door open and stepped into the darkened living room. Situated on the second floor of an old mansion converted into six individual residences, the apartment was more spacious than many on the island. The long, narrow living area was flanked on one side by the three bedrooms, all of which opened into it. The balcony at the front of the house had been converted into a small eating nook and a barely adequate kitchen. The single bath occupied one corner of the rear balcony, leaving them a precious, if tiny, spot to park a lawn chair and hang a potted plant. The center bedroom belonged to Amber and Linda, the one nearest the bath and balcony to Sharon, the one next to the kitchen to Walt. Automatically, Amber reached for the wall switch and flipped on the overhead light.

A strange man stretched out full-length on the couch lifted his head and looked at her. Amber gasped and stepped back. The next instant, Sharon shoved up on one elbow and turned a look over her shoulder. Sharon's big brown eyes rolled as the man scrambled off of her and into a sitting position.

"Damn, Amber," Sharon drawled huskily. "Don't you believe in knocking?"

Amber fought down the heat of embarrassment and dropped her bundle. "I live here. This is a communal room. And you didn't even lock the door."

"Lock the door, lock the door," Sharon parroted, stretching her arms languidly over her head. The man cleared his throat and rubbed his nose. Sharon smiled wryly, then pulled down her blouse and sat up. Her long dark brown hair was mussed, and the scooped neckline of her top showed a bright purple hickey on her collarbone. Amber looked away. She couldn't believe how little self-respect Sharon displayed. These tawdry scenes were becoming all too familiar.

"Excuse me," she said, bending to retrieve her bundle. "I'm going to bed."

"Alone," Sharon purred. "Amber always goes to bed alone," she told the man beside her. "She's such a good girl."

Amber moved swiftly around the couch and toward her bedroom door while Sharon laughed.

"I prefer bad girls," the man rasped, pulling Sharon's head toward his with both hands.

"You and every other man in town," Amber muttered beneath her breath while Sharon laughed throatily.

"Oh, Amber!" Sharon called just as Amber's hand fell on the doorknob.

Amber paused but said nothing.

"Your hair dryer's fried," Sharon informed her. "Sorry."

Amber whirled around. She'd about had it with the other woman invading her private space and taking anything she wanted. "What do you know about my hair dryer?"

Sharon shrugged, one hand sliding across the man's chest and downward. "I borrowed it," she said innocently.

"Why is it that everything of mine you 'borrow' winds up ruined?"

"Does it?" Sharon asked with such patent falseness that Amber wanted to smack her. "Wouldn't happen if you didn't buy such cheap stuff," Sharon needled. She bent her head close to her companion's then and whispered in his ear. He chuckled and slid down on the couch, pulling her down with him.

Amber immediately turned away and shoved open the door to her bedroom. To her surprise, Linda lay atop the twin bed Amber had installed for her, reading beneath the meager light of a bedside lamp. She sat up, pushing her short, pale blond hair off of her face. Amber quickly closed the door behind her.

"Are they still out there?" Linda asked.

Amber sighed inwardly. "Yes."

Linda made a face. "Why don't they go to the bedroom?"

Amber frowned. "Sharon likes to shock us. That's why."

Linda nodded, her hair falling forward again. She looked up from beneath her shaggy bangs. "He's kind of cute, don't you think?"

"Who?"

"That guy with Sharon."

Amber could only stare at the girl. "I didn't notice, frankly."

"Well, I thought he was kind of cute."

Amber tossed her bundle onto her own bed, which she had shoved up into the corner to make room for Linda's. "I hope you aren't thinking of trying to snag his attention."

"Oh, no." Linda slid back into the center of the bed, pulling up her bare feet to tuck them beneath her. "I know I can't compete with Sharon."

"That's not what I meant." Amber dropped down onto the side of her own bed and looked at the tall, thin blonde. "Any man who would do what he's doing isn't worthy of you."

Linda smiled, but then she shrugged. "Any guy'll take it if he can get it."

"Not any guy," Amber argued, "not Walt, and you know she's offered."

Linda shrugged again and looked away but not before Amber noted the light of interest in her pale blue eyes. "Anyway," Linda said, "I don't even know his name."

"I doubt Sharon does either," Amber said smartly, then immediately regretted it. "I just don't get her. Doesn't she have any self-respect? Why does she do this to herself?"

Linda swivelled and laid back on her pillow, stretching out her long, slender legs. "Maybe she thinks she has to," she said softly.

Amber wondered if the girl was talking about Sharon or herself. She feared it was the latter. "Listen to me," Amber urged. "No one has to sleep around to be liked or to be popular or to get a guy."

"You sure don't," Linda muttered.

"No, I don't," Amber agreed. "And neither do you."

Linda said nothing, just picked up her book from the bedside table and held it in front of her face. Amber bit her lip, wondering if she should say more. Eventually, remembering the many tiresome lectures she herself had received, she decided that it would do more harm than good. Silently, she hung up her costume and began preparing for bed, more depressed than ever.

Chapter Three

Amber kicked back the covers and rolled onto her side, rising up to punch her pillow. She settled down again, let out a long breath and closed her eyes. Muffled laughter from the room next door set her teeth on edge. They'd been at it all night, those two, and as loudly as they could manage, it seemed to her. She rolled again, so restless that her skin felt jumpy and prickly. Determinedly, she closed her eyes. When she heard a faint moan, she put her hands over her ears.

Why was this happening? She was dead tired, but for some reason she couldn't sleep, couldn't lock out the murmurs and rustling and distant cries in the night. Perhaps it had to do with the fact that every time she drifted down to sleep, a dream of steamy passion overtook her, but the faces she saw were not those of Sharon and her stranger. They were her own and that of Reece Carlyle.

In the dream, she felt his hand clamped around her wrist, slowly drawing her to him, saw the crinkles at the outer edges of those dreamy eyes, knew that he was going to kiss her with those finely drawn lips. Her heart pounded as if she'd been running for miles. Something clutched deep in the pit of her belly, and she pressed her legs together involuntarily. It was both intense and disturbing, unlike any other dream she'd ever had, and while she wanted to sleep, she didn't want to visit that dream again and could only wonder why she'd had it.

Perhaps she'd been so intent for so long on getting together the funds to leave this place that she hadn't been paying enough attention to her other needs. Maybe Walt was right and she just needed to have some fun. Or maybe now that her goal was within sight—a few more months at the most—her mind was naturally turning to other things, like handsome, windblown flirts with sexy smiles.

Someone in the next room cried out hoarsely, and Amber bolted straight up in bed. Suddenly she just couldn't stand it anymore. The four walls seemed to be closing in around her. She couldn't breathe, couldn't think. In the bed across the room, Linda lay motionless, silent, asleep. Drawing her knees up, Amber bowed her head over them and forced herself to reason.

This situation was insane, but she could do something to make it better, surely. But what? Warm milk might make her drowsy, but she'd have to go into the kitchen for it, and Sharon and her lover had been in and out of there several times during the course of the evening, usually for cold beers, and the last thing Amber wanted to do was run into either of them. A long soak in a hot tub often relaxed her, but it was already sultry enough that the idea didn't appeal. Soft, dreamy music sometimes put her out; unfortunately the sound system belonged to Walt and he'd moved it into his room after Sharon had blown one of his speakers. He'd always encouraged Amber to make use of it, but since he'd turned in long ago and was presumably sleeping, she couldn't do so now. She could turn on the bedside lamp and read a book, but that might wake Linda. The only other remedy she could think of was a long walk.

A glance at the clock showed her that morning was not far away. She could go for a walk, or perhaps a bike ride, then return to the apartment for a few hours of sleep before she had to visit the laundromat and pay her bills. No one else around here would be up before noon, if then. As quietly as possible, she rose and dressed in shorts, tank top and a loose, long-sleeve blouse before brushing her hair up into a ponytail and securing it with a puffy rubber band. Tucking her small wallet and keys into her pockets, she carried her tennis shoes out to the landing on the stairway. She locked the apartment, then sat on the top step to put on and tie her shoes. That done, she went down the steps.

The bike was kept stored beneath the stairwell, and she struggled with the combination lock on the chain, wishing she'd brought a flashlight with her. Finally, the tumblers clicked and she was able to separate the bike chain, drape it over her shoulder and roll the bike out from beneath the stairs. She pushed it out to the street, mounted, and headed south toward the wharf at a sedate, lazy pace. As she pedaled, the softness of the night enveloped her, calming her nerves and soothing her mind. She inhaled the clean air, at peace finally.

Sunsets were a big deal in Key West. Every evening a significant portion of the population gathered at Mallory Square on the western side of the southern point of the island to watch the sun sink into the ocean. Sunset sails were popular among the tourists, and the locals debated the legendary "green flash" rumored to occur at irregular intervals. Personally, Amber preferred the sunrise. So she decided upon the eastern end of the Boardwalk. But she was in no hurry. Sunrise was yet an hour away.

She wandered the streets, turning corners simply because they were there, loving the solitude, absorbing the peace. Eventually, she found herself at the boardwalk. Pleasantly tired, she chained the bike to a post and strolled onto the wharf, listening to her own footsteps and the gentle lapping of the water as the sky gradually lightened. When she reached the eastern end of the pier, she sat down, removed her shoes and dangled her feet over the edge, swinging her legs easily so that her toes skimmed the chilly surface of the water, kicking up droplets to sparkle in the light of a nearby beacon and plink softly back into the ocean. Gradually, gold gilded the edge of the horizon, sparking the water and slowly setting it ablaze. Amber folded her arms over the bottom rung of the wooden fence surrounding the wharf and propped her chin atop them, content.

Reece propped his feet on the metal rail and leaned back with an audible sigh, a cup of strong, black, fragrant coffee in his hands. He loved the morning and never more so than when at sea. Watching the sun slowly climb above the horizon and paint the sea platinum was a special joy that never failed to bring him peace. He couldn't get the whole effect sitting in harbor, of course, but he still adored this time before the rest of the world awoke. That was especially true here in Key West, where the sunset signaled happy hour. Absently, he looked toward the pier across the harbor, and movement at the eastern end snagged his attention. So he was not the only one here who enjoyed this particular time of day, after all. Curious who else in this party town might share his predilection, he got up and moved to the pilothouse. Opening a small compartment, he removed a pair of binoculars and trained them on the pier.

He set down his coffee cup abruptly. "I don't believe it."

He quickly refocused the binoculars. If that wasn't Amber Presley, he'd eat his shoes. Turned resolutely toward the east, she sat with her chin parked atop her folded arms, looking through the waist-high barricade that surrounded the wharf. She turned her head then, presenting him a clear view of her face, and something jolted inside his chest.

Perhaps that face was too round to be considered classically beautiful, but those enormous eyes, that small, upturned nose and a plump, cupid's bow of a mouth made him smile. He noted the slight arch and graceful sweep of her brows and the strength of her chin and jawline. Lowering the binoculars, he remembered the smooth, pale gold of her skin and the light golden brown of her eyes. Combined with the sumptuous red highlights of her medium-brown hair and the dusty pink of her mouth, she reminded him more of the sunset than the sunrise, but he had no doubt from her expression that she enjoyed the awe of morning as much as he. The discovery afforded him an opportunity that he was not foolish enough to waste.

He left the coffee where it was and ignored the rumbling of his stomach as he hurried below to grab his wallet from his bunk before rushing back up top again. Moving to the rail, he carefully stepped over it and descended the ladder to the small skiff tied below. With sure, practiced movements, he started the tiny outboard trolling motor and steered the rudder toward the pier.

The boarding break in the barricade was in the very center of the wharf, so Reece headed the skiff there and moored it alongside a walk jutting out into the harbor. This he followed swiftly to the wharf. His topsiders squeaked over the planks as he moved toward the east. As he drew near, he slowed, oddly entranced by the delicate line of her spine beneath the thin layers of cotton.

The first rays of sunshine reflecting off the water's surface rendered the overblouse all but invisible, leaving the darker shades of tank top and shorts clearly delineated. Her shoulders seemed broader from this angle, her waist quite small and tightly cinched, hips flaring into rounded fullness. Somehow, the shape was more womanly than he'd expected. He shook that thought away, reminding himself that she was little more than a child, really, and fixed his attention on the plump ponytail swinging from the back of her head. A child, a very pretty child. Decidedly more comfortable with that thought, he smiled and moved forward.

Amber registered dimly the squeak of rubber on wood but didn't realize that it signaled approach until someone dropped down on the end of the pier beside her. Jerking around, she rocked over onto one thigh, putting distance between herself and the interloper. Her shock must have registered plainly, for the smile on his face broke into laughter.

"You!" Reece Carlyle. Gilded and polished by the sunrise, the man was a sight to behold. For a moment she could only gape, wondering if she'd conjured him from her dreams.

"Good morning." He beamed, as bright as any sunray.

She found herself infected by that smile, melted by it, warmed. "Uh, good morning. I, um, didn't expect anyone else to be about."

He settled beside her, tanned legs folded beneath the hems of pale blue shorts, and sucked in a deep breath. "Oh, I love morning. It's the best time of day. Especially mornings like this. Don't you agree?"

She found herself nodding. The thought followed belatedly that she had again allowed him to engage her. Prudence dictated that she get up and walk away, but she couldn't seem to find the will to do so. She slumped, wondering why it should be so, why she wanted to talk to him. It wasn't smart. After all, she knew nothing whatsoever about this man other than his name. Her natural inclination was toward caution; yet, she couldn't deny that she wanted to spend a little time with him, just a little time. She hung her chin on the edge of the plank in front of her and squinted into the morning sun as it crept diligently above the horizon.

"I saw you from my boat," he said, surprisingly close to her ear. He lifted a hand and pointed toward a sleek cabin cruiser in the distance. "That's it out there, the *Merry Haven*."

She was surprised at the size of it, forty feet at least. "You sail her alone?"

"I do. Everything's fully mechanized, and she's perfectly rigged, but I'm careful, not taking any chances. I have nothing to prove, just giving myself some time on my own. I've been sailing around the Gulf of Mexico for almost three months now, and I've allotted myself another three months before I return to the real world."

She turned her head and studied him, her cheek resting against her forearm. The morning light certainly showed him to good advantage. He sat there, cleanly shaven and sun-gilded, his streaked hair curling against the nape of his neck. The hairs on his tanned, muscular legs and arms were blond from constant exposure to the sun. Even his straight, slender brows were tipped with gold. She studied his face. He had strong, regular features, deeply set eyes that fairly glowed with good health, their irises an intriguing combination of green, gold and blue bits. She found no guile in those eyes, only gentleness and interest. Nothing to prove, indeed.

"You don't give up easily, do you?" she observed.

He smiled and looked down at his crossed ankles. "Not easily, no."

But he had given up, sometime, on someone. She could hear it in his voice, felt his regret. She turned her gaze back to his boat, half expecting an invitation to visit it with him, wondering what had compelled him to devote six months to such a solitary existence. The thought occurred that the man might actually be lonely; yet she sensed a kind of peace about him that frankly appealed to her. She pondered that, absorbed a little of it as she let her gaze wander back to the sunrise. Lifting a hand, she shaded her eyes. Three-quarters of the blazing orb had already risen above the sea. She watched a few minutes longer, amazed at how obviously the change occurred. The lower edge of the sun had barely risen above the line of the horizon when he laid a hand over the board close to her elbow.

"Say, you wouldn't know where a fellow could get a really good cup of coffee around here, would you, and maybe a bite of breakfast to go with it?"

Not an invitation out to the boat then. She smiled at that. "Sure." Twisting at the waist, she pointed toward the west, sunlight dancing before her eyes as they adjusted. "Just follow the boardwalk all the way to Front Street. Turn left on Simonton, and before you get to Fleming you'll see the sidewalk tables. It's just a storefront, no inside dining, but there's a covered deck, and the food is good. But now the coffee, ah, the coffee is marvelous. And the doughnuts are to die for."

He laughed. "Sounds perfect. But, um, Front Street? I don't remember that Front Street connects with the boardwalk."

"Well, not exactly, no, but—"

He got up suddenly, just planted his feet and pushed himself right up to a standing position. "Why don't you show me?" he asked, offering her a hand. "There'll be a good breakfast in it for you—unless the food's not as fine as you say."

He grinned a challenge down at her, but it was backed

up by a genuine hopefulness that both flattered and intrigued. She found herself smiling in reply, and then her hand just naturally settled into his, and he was pulling her up to her feet. He released her immediately and linked his hands together behind his back. Pivoting smartly on his heel, he waited until she fell in beside him, then started off down the boardwalk at a stroll. When they reached the ramp, she remembered her bike.

"We can come back for it later," he said helpfully.

She bit her lip. Later. That implied something more than breakfast, didn't it? Or was she reading more into it than was there? He seemed to know her thoughts. He chuckled and shook his head.

"I've been on that boat alone for three months," he said, "and it's been good for me, but right now I want a little company and some conversation. And that's all. But if you think you might have to make a quick getaway from a public place, then by all means, take the bike."

A quick getaway. From a public place. By bike, no less. When he put it that way, it sounded flatly absurd. Which it was. She was in complete control here, after all. He didn't even know where they were going. They would be sitting on the sidewalk in plain view. Her lips quirked with a spontaneous smile.

"I guess I'm just a cautious sort."

He grinned at her. "I noticed. And, for what it's worth, I approve."

She tilted her head. "Do you?"

"Certainly. It's smart to be cautious. I've worked hard to teach my daughter that very point."

A daughter. So he was married—or had been. "You have a daughter?"

His smile displayed definite pride. "Her name is Brittany. She's eleven, brilliant, beautiful and a real handful.

She lives with her mom, but I'm going to have her with me on the boat for a full month before school starts.''

An absurd relief flooded her. ''You're divorced.''

''Yes. For over a year now.'' The regret rang through again.

''I'm sorry.''

''So am I, but it was a mutual decision and the best thing to do.'' He folded his arms. ''Now, how about that breakfast? I'm starving.''

She nodded and turned away from the bike. They strolled along a few moments in silence. Then Reece turned to her with a raised eyebrow. ''So, tell me about yourself, Amber Rose.''

''What do you want to know?''

''Well, for starters, how did you come to be here in Key West?''

She grimaced, but she answered without even wondering if she should. ''Sheer stupidity, I'm afraid, along with a heavy dollop of immaturity.''

He looked surprised, but then he laughed. ''Doesn't sound like a permanent condition, but it does require a little explanation, if you don't mind.''

The funny thing was, she didn't mind at all. ''I grew up in Texas,'' she began, ''but I went to college in New York state, where it was cold and snowed a lot. I graduated midterm, by the way.''

''When it was cold and snowing a lot,'' he put in astutely.

She grinned. ''Yeah. Anyway, I couldn't go home, so when some friends suggested we all come down to Key West to celebrate and escape the winter, I thought it was a pretty good idea.''

''What do you mean you *couldn't* go home?'' he asked carefully.

She shrugged, swinging her arms at her sides as they

walked. "Just that. I couldn't go back to my parents' home. I couldn't—can't—even move close to them."

"Why is that?" he pressed. "I mean, it's none of my business, of course, but, speaking personally, I'd be crushed if my daughter didn't want to live close to me."

"Then don't try to live her life for her," Amber said flatly. "Don't tell her who she can have for friends and who she can't. Don't tell her where she can work and what she can wear and who she should and shouldn't date and what kind of music she can listen to and what to do with her own money and when to go to bed and when to get up again and how to breathe...." She broke off and heaved a deep sigh.

Reece spread his hands. "But that's pretty much what parents do for their children, isn't it? I certainly police my daughter's activities and monitor her schedule and guide her friendships."

"Yes, but your daughter's eleven. I'm twenty-four."

"And when was the last time you saw your parents?"

"At graduation."

"They must be heartbroken," Reece said, shaking his head.

"I've tried to tell them that I'm all right," she told him defensively, "but every conversation deteriorates into a shouting match with my father demanding I come home to live and me insisting that I won't."

He waved a hand as if to say that this was incidental or unimportant. "Let's go back to the part where you were coming down to Key West to celebrate and get away from the winter weather. How did you wind up staying?"

She made a face. "My father made a huge deal about the trip. He was sure I was going to get drunk and drown myself—or worse. I think I pretty much intended to prove him right."

"And did you?"

"Well, it was quite a party," she admitted, "but when it was all over with, nothing had changed. Then it came time to leave, and I just didn't have anywhere to go. The weather at that time of year was glorious, and a girlfriend of mine had met a guy who offered us both a place to stay, so we did."

"And where is she now?"

"Oh, it didn't work out between them, and after a couple weeks she went back to her home in New Jersey. I had a job by then, receptionist at a real estate office, which was how I found my first apartment. But it was just too expensive. It took every cent I could make to pay the bills, and I began to realize that I didn't really want to be here."

"And that was how long ago?" he asked.

"Oh, two years. Well, two and a half. I knew within four or five months that I'd made a mistake."

"But you're still here," he pointed out needlessly.

"And will be for several more months."

He stopped in his tracks and lifted his hands to his hips. "I don't understand."

He couldn't, of course, so she explained it to him. "First, I had to wait out my lease. Then I had to find a new place and roommates. I had changed jobs by then, but that wasn't enough to start saving, so I found a second job and set up a budget. I've been saving steadily for the past nineteen, twenty months, but it's so expensive here that it takes a long time to put together enough to start over. Take the cost of transportation. We're at the southern tip of the U.S. I don't have a car. A one-way airline ticket to Miami is two hundred bucks. And I don't intend to stay in Miami. Add to that the fact that I came to Key West with what I could pack in a single suitcase. All I own are shorts and jeans."

"And a witch costume," he pointed out with a small smile.

"Very helpful," she admitted drolly. "The point is, I have to be able to purchase a suitable wardrobe in order to begin interviewing for jobs in the real world. Then there's the cost of finding and renting a place to live. No telling how long that will take. I have to be prepared to spend a few weeks in a hotel. And there's transportation costs to consider. I'll probably have to buy a car. And then there's food and furniture and, well, you get the picture."

Nodding thoughtfully, he turned them down the sidewalk once more, hands sliding into the pockets of his shorts. "It would be a lot easier if you'd just go home."

"Easier?" she scoffed. "Believe me, it would be anything but."

"Surely your parents would help you get started again," he argued gently.

"It's not up to my parents to help me get started again," she replied firmly. "Would you expect your parents to help you get started again?"

He lifted a hand to the back of his neck. "Well, no, but…"

"But nothing," she insisted. "I'm an adult, and if I allow my father to think anything else, even for a moment, I might as well go back to pinafores and pigtails. He's a very strong-willed man, and I admit that I have a difficult time standing up to him, so I have no choice but to keep my distance." She shook her head. "No, I have to do this on my own. I *will* do this on my own. I hope eventually that he'll accept me as I am and we can have a real relationship, but until I'm well established, I don't dare go home again. And that's all there is to it."

For a moment, she thought he might argue the point, but then he smiled, rubbed his flat middle with one hand and said playfully, "Please tell me we're close to breakfast."

Laughing, she pointed down the street. "Think you can make it two more blocks?"

"I'll try," he said mournfully, dragging his feet as if terribly weakened. "If I don't make it, just bury me at sea."

"I'm not hauling your carcass all the way back to the wharf," she exclaimed, taking off at a trot.

"Hey!" He flashed by her, then turned and trotted backward. "Some friend you're turning out to be."

"Got you moving, didn't I?"

He stopped dead in his tracks. Laughing, she jogged past him. "Okay," he called out, "no coffee for you. You're entirely too frisky this morning."

She just kept going, secretly pleased to have been labeled his friend. A moment later he caught up with her. Jogging at her side, he looked down and asked, tongue in cheek, "Anybody ever tell you that you're just no fun?"

"All the time."

"Well, they lied," he said, flashing that brilliant smile.

She laughed as he sped away from her. When he got to the corner, he stopped and waited, comically expressing impatience with huffs and tapping toes and rolling eyes. Conversely, the closer she got, the slower Amber moved, until she was the one dragging her feet ludicrously. As soon as she drew near enough, he grabbed her by the hand and hauled her across the street, laughing. When they hit the curb, they were both running flat out. A short block later, she drew up. He raced past her, his hand still gripping hers, then swung back at the end of her arm, so that they collided gently, stumbling slightly, feet tangling, chests heaving. He wrapped an arm around her shoulders, steadying them both as they caught their breath. Amber looked up, smiling, a witty quip on the end of her tongue. It faded into oblivion at the expression on his face.

Part confusion, part shock and part something else she

couldn't quite define, he seemed momentarily frozen in the expression of it. His brows drew together, his lips parted, and all the while his eyes plumbed hers. When his gaze dropped to her mouth, she inwardly gasped, certain suddenly that he was thinking of kissing her. The next instant, he dropped his arm and jerked back, clearing his throat.

"I'm so hungry I'm stupid," he mumbled.

She looked away, got her bearings and moved purposefully through the wooden railings that were flanked on one side by a covered deck and on the other side by tables set on the grass and shaded with umbrellas. "Well, if you can make it as far as the order window, you're saved," she told him blithely.

Behind her, he inhaled deeply. "Oh, just smell that coffee."

Chuckling, she greeted the dark man behind the open window. "Morning, Alonso."

"Morning, Amber, honey. How are you today?"

"I'm fine. My friend here is about to collapse from starvation."

"Well, we can sure fix that up quick. What you having?"

"Two coffees to start. And I want two of those chocolate doughnuts you do so well." She turned to Reece, who was studying the menu taped to the window. "What about you?" she asked as Alonso quickly poured two tall insulated cups of his special Colombian blend.

"I want something a little heartier than doughnuts," Reece told her. As Alonso set the cups on the counter, Reece looked to him. "I'll have the shrimp omelet, cheese biscuits, hashbrowns and a side of brown sugar bacon."

Alonso lifted an eyebrow at Amber, who lifted an eyebrow at Reece. "What?" he asked. "I always eat a big breakfast, and this morning I'm really hungry."

Amber turned to Alonso. "You heard the man."

"Um-mm-mm," Alonso said, grabbing his skillet. "I do love a man who can eat." He blew a kiss at Reece and whirled toward a basket of eggs.

Amber schooled a smile, knowing well Alonso's particular proclivities. The island supported a substantial gay population. Reece backed up a step, cleared his throat and pretended not to notice that Alonso was making eyes at him over his mixing bowl. Amber shoved his coffee at him. "Cream and sugar on the sideboard."

"I take mine black," he told her, gingerly removing the cup from her hand. He swirled the black liquid, then lifted the cup to his lips, sipping appreciatively. "Mmm, excellent."

"Told you. Let's sit down. Alonso will ring the bell when our order's ready." She led the way to a table on the deck. He quickly stepped around her and pulled out the simple lawn chair for her to sit. Unaccustomed to such gentlemanly behavior, she flashed him a surprised look before lowering herself into the chair. He pulled out the one next to her and sat, crossing his long, muscular legs and inhaling his coffee.

"I can't believe we're the only ones here," he said, glancing around. "The coffee alone ought to have them lining up in droves."

"Key West is not a morning town," she told him, sipping from her own cup. "He does a brisk Sunday brunch trade, though, and in the afternoons he switches to sandwiches and frozen drinks."

"Well, I, for one, am glad he's open for breakfast."

"Me, too." She sipped her coffee for a few minutes, watching him gulp his, then offered to get him a refill.

He waved that away and set aside his cup. "No, I'll wait for the meal."

"In that case, why don't you tell me about yourself? We've only talked about me so far."

He shrugged. "Not much to tell. I'm a native Texan, like you."

She lifted an unsurprised brow. "I did recognize the accent."

He grinned. "I grew up in Corpus Christi, went to college in Houston, made that my base of operations, and I guess it's home now, though I don't actually have a place there anymore. We sold the house, the business, everything, in the property settlement."

"Must've been hard, giving up everything you'd worked for."

"Not nearly so hard as giving up full-time residence with my daughter." He waved a hand. "The house itself was nothing, really. The business, though, that was tough."

"What sort of business?" she asked.

"Computer technology support."

She shook her head apologetically. "My degree is in theater, with a minor in English. A computer is a glorified typewriter, as far as I'm concerned."

He leaned in closer, warming to the subject. "A lot of people are the same way, people in business. Even the computer literate have a hard time keeping up with all the innovations and advances. That's where I come in. I put together a crack research team. We knew what was coming before the developers did. Then I sold that knowledge and taught its application to businesses who needed to update or make the most of what they already had. We studied a firm's needs and advised on new purchases, taught software use, that sort of thing. Sometimes we even went to the manufacturers on behalf of our clients with ideas on how they could tailor their products to meet certain needs. Pretty soon, the manufacturers were coming to us."

"Sounds exciting."

"Oh, it is. Was." He cleared his throat. "Actually, it

was one of the manufacturers who bought us out. The problem now is that I don't know what to do next. I signed a non-competition agreement, so it will mean starting all over. I'm not too old at thirty-eight to start over in business. I just don't know what I want to start over in." He sighed. "That's what I'm doing here. I decided to take six months to get my head together, you know?"

She smiled ruefully. "I know too well," she admitted. "I've been getting myself together for twenty-four years now."

He chuckled at that. "Hey, don't rush it. I married at twenty-four—and lived to regret it, believe me. Except for my daughter. Her I'll never regret."

"You say she's eleven?"

"That's right."

"So you were a father by twenty-seven."

"Yes."

She looked into her cup. "I wonder if I'll be a mother by twenty-seven."

"Do you want to be?"

She tilted her head to the side, thinking about it. "Yes, I think I do. I've always loved kids. In fact, I have decided that I want to teach."

"Oh, really? What subject?"

"Life," she answered, then expounded. "I'd like to teach theater to underprivileged or problem children."

"The theater-as-a-microcosm-of-life thing?" he asked dubiously.

She wrinkled her nose. "More theater-as-a-tool-for-personal-growth. It's so much more than acting, building sets, integrating light and sound and movement. Theater teaches confidence to the shy, discipline to the extrovert, grace to the awkward, the joy of the fantastic to the un-imaginative…. The possibilities are limitless, frankly, and the sad part is that those most in need of that kind of experience have the least opportunity for it.''

He seemed to be considering that when the bell clanged and Alonso leaned out the window to shout, ''Yoo-hoo! Chow's ready.''

Reece shot a worried glance toward the window, but Amber was already pushing back her chair. ''I'll get it,'' she told him laughingly.

''Thanks. Oh, wait!'' He stood and pulled his wallet from his pocket. ''I'm paying, remember?''

''That's not necessary.''

''Sure it is.'' He shoved a twenty at her. ''I insist. That was the deal. You showed me the way, I buy your breakfast.''

She shrugged. ''Okay.''

Grinning, he folded the twenty into her palm and leaned close to whisper, ''You get a tip if you can distract the cook.''

''I'm not his type,'' she whispered back.

''Neither am I. That's the point.''

Laughing, she turned away. It occurred to her as she was waiting for the change that she hadn't laughed so much in a very long time.

Chapter Four

"That was marvelous," he said, patting his full belly. "Now I really have to walk it off."

Amber got up from her chair and began gathering the refuse. He got up, too, and began helping her, his big hands covering hers. "Here, I'll do this. You served, after all."

Finding the contact oddly disturbing, she backed up a step and folded her arms. "Fine. Knock yourself out."

He got everything together, placed it all on the tray and carried it to the trash barrel set out for that purpose. He emptied the tray and placed it on the counter. "You come back now," Alonso called from inside.

Reece waved and smiled. "Not alone," he murmured through his teeth. Amber chuckled behind her hand. He wheeled around, grinning sheepishly, and jerked a thumb toward the pavement. "Quick, before he starts blowing kisses again," he muttered.

She saluted smartly and hurried toward the street. He caught up with her and linked his arm with hers to slow her down. "Where's the fire?"

She pointed overhead. "It's beginning to heat up."

"All the more reason to take it easy," he said.

"Especially if you just gorged yourself," she teased.

He hung his head in an admission of guilt. "It wasn't my fault. I was starving. And he heaped my plate with all that good food."

She laughed. "He likes you."

Reece chuckled. "Well, I'll say this for the fellow, he can cook."

"He certainly can."

They strolled arm in arm for a moment, then she said, "He did actually serve you more food than normal."

Reece groaned. "I knew it."

"But I didn't see anyone holding a gun on you to make you eat it all."

"I'm a weak man," Reece moaned in a delightfully silly voice. She put her head back and laughed. He laughed with her, even as he asked, "What's so funny?"

"You are. A weak man does not accomplish all that you have accomplished by thirty-eight."

He shrugged. "Oh, I don't know. Thirty-eight years is a long time."

She scoffed at that. "It depends on the perspective, now doesn't it?"

"I suppose." He unhooked his arm from hers.

"What about the rest of your family?" she asked, realizing suddenly that he'd said nothing about anyone but his daughter and ex-wife. "Parents, siblings, that sort of thing."

"My folks are still in Corpus Christi," he told her. "My dad's a retired postal worker. My younger brother, Caleb, and his family are there, too. He has two boys. Our older brother, Jason, is in Galveston. He just married, finally, and is expecting his first, but he has two stepchildren, a boy and a girl, who he is just crazy about."

"So you're the middle brother."

"Yep. We're two years apart, each of us, more or less."

"That means Jason's forty."

"Just."

"And Caleb's thirty-six."

"He'll be thirty-seven exactly one month before I'm thirty-nine."

"And that will be when?"

"December for him, January for me, the tenth."

"Oh! Mine's the tenth, too, of February."

"No kidding? December, January, February."

"December and January birthdays must be hard," Amber said, just making small talk, "with the Christmas holidays and all."

"A little, when we were boys, not so much now," he told her. "Anyway, you've got Valentine's right around your birthday."

"Hasn't been a problem," she admitted dryly.

He seemed to study her for a moment. "Your boyfriend hasn't ever tried to combine the two?"

She chuckled. "Nope."

"He hasn't ever tried to sell you on one big present instead of two?"

"No."

"Because some guys, they try to do that, you know. It's not necessarily that they're cheap, though it could be that, of course. It's more that they don't know how to shop for a woman and so it's this big ordeal for them, in which case, they sometimes try to, you know, combine."

This was obviously a matter he'd given lots of thought. Grinning, she shook her head and finally admitted, "Look, I don't have a boyfriend, okay? But I'll keep that in mind."

He rubbed the back of his neck again. "You really don't have a boyfriend?"

He made it sound as if that fact was hard to believe, and she felt a tiny surge of delight at the prospect. "No boyfriend," she confirmed succinctly.

He paused an instant and then asked, "What about the taxi driver?"

She'd forgotten that he'd seen her with Walt yesterday. A little deflated, she said, "Oh, he's not my boyfriend. What makes you think he's my boyfriend?"

"The way he talked to you for one thing. He called you 'Babe.'"

She waved that away, absently following as he turned the corner. "Oh, Walt always does that. It doesn't mean anything."

"I, um, I heard you say something about home. It, um, sounded like you live together."

"Well, we do live together," she said frankly. "He's one of my roommates."

"One of your roommates?"

"Sure. There are four of us in a three-bedroom apartment."

"Which, um, means that someone shares a bedroom with someone else," he pointed out carefully.

She stopped where she was and stared at him, a little insulted. "I share a bedroom with a friend from work. Her name is Linda. Walt has his own bedroom, as does our other roomie, Sharon."

Reece stared at her for a long moment. "Then Walt is just your roommate," he said.

She threw up her arms. "That's what I said!"

"I-I'm sorry, I just... Well, he seemed like a boyfriend, that's all."

"Do you think I'd be having breakfast with you if I had a boyfriend?" she demanded.

He blinked at her. "Well, why not? That is, I don't think

he, er, a boyfriend, would necessarily see it, rather, me, as a threat, ah, given the age difference."

"What age difference?" she asked, truly stymied.

He blinked again. "I'm fourteen years older than you."

"What has that got to do with anything?"

He opened his mouth, then closed it again. For a long moment he stared off into the distance. Finally he took a deep breath and said, "Fourteen years, well, some people might think that's a lot."

"I can't imagine why," she said. "I mean, it's not like we aren't both adults."

He seemed thoroughly confused for a moment. Then he smiled weakly and said, "Right."

She started walking again. "I don't know anyone who would make a big deal about something like that," she said, "except maybe my father. But he'd find an objection no matter."

"Ah."

"Certainly no one around here would think anything of it. This is the town with the clothing optional bars."

"No way." He sounded truly shocked.

"Way."

He shook his head. "No wonder you want out of here."

She shrugged. "I just don't fit in, you know?"

"I can see that."

"The problem is, I don't really know where I want to go. What about you?" she asked, feeling that there were some similarities in their situations. They were both running away, after all, she from an overbearing father, he from a failed marriage.

"I, um, don't follow."

"Where will you go after you've gotten yourself together?"

He lifted an eyebrow at that. "Oh. Back to Houston."

"Even though that's where your ex is?"

"It's also where my daughter is."

"Right. Of course. But what if she was grown and didn't need you anymore?"

He clasped his hands together behind his back, obviously thinking about it. "Well, I like Texas, and there's lots of business opportunity in Houston. That's what I know. Yes, I'd go back to Houston."

"Not Corpus Christi?"

He shook his head. "Not the same business climate."

"What about Dallas?"

"Possibility," he said, "but Houston is closer to my folks."

"San Antonio?"

"I really like to be near the ocean."

She nodded. Sounded perfectly logical.

"What about you?" he asked. "Will you go back to Texas?"

She'd tussled with that question repeatedly and still had no real answer. "I might. I've thought about the northeast, but I really hate the cold. So then I think West Coast, but..."

"Texas is what you know," he said helpfully.

She nodded. "Exactly."

"So maybe you'll go back to Dallas after all."

"No, not Dallas," she told him flatly. "San Antonio, maybe."

"Or Houston?"

"Maybe. Or El Paso."

"Amarillo?"

"You're forgetting those—"

"Cold winters," he interrupted, eyes twinkling, demonstrating that he hadn't forgotten at all.

"Exactly."

They walked on, talking and teasing. The subject eventually turned to the eccentricities of Key West, and that brought lots of reasons for laughter, since the island literally reveled in its oddities. Before she realized it, the morning had disappeared and Amber found herself standing, not at the wharf or anywhere near it but many blocks to the south and east at Jose Marti Street near Duncan, not half a block from her own apartment! She dropped the conversation flat and simply gaped at the stairs climbing the side of the building, where Walt sat bent over some project or other.

Reece Carlyle looked around and asked, "What is it?"

"I'm home."

"What?"

She pointed to the old house that contained her apartment. "I wasn't paying attention, and I guess I just wandered home. What time is it anyway?"

Reece checked his watch, reared back and announced, "Half past twelve!"

They gaped at each other, then they laughed. Time had certainly gotten away from them. He wiped perspiration from his forehead, and she suddenly became aware of the droplets rolling down the cleft between her breasts. She'd shrugged out of the overblouse sometime earlier and tied it around her waist. Now she plucked at the knit top, fanning herself with one hand.

"We left your bike at the wharf," Reece said, and Amber groaned, thinking about the long walk back there and the ride, in the heat of the day, back here. Forget the laundry.

"I'll get it later," she decided unhappily, "after I've cooled down."

He nodded and slid a look at Walt. "Tell you what, it's just a suggestion now, a way to beat the heat and get your bike, too, s-sort of killing two birds with one stone."

Amber smiled. Just as he had the day before when trying to ask her out, he was being endearingly awkward about this, whatever this was. "I'm not much for killing birds," she quipped wryly, "but I'm always interested in beating the heat."

He tossed another look at Walt. "I was thinking about a swim, not in the harbor, of course. You can't swim in the harbor, so, I, um, thought we could take the boat out of the cove, you know, past the reef, maybe. Water's cool out there, and, um, I wouldn't go by myself, not to swim, but if you were to come along, that'd be okay, safe. Don't you think?"

She'd had much more shocking propositions put to her in much smoother fashion, and she found herself liking his nervous uncertainty a great deal. It was refreshing, especially in such a great-looking guy. She wondered if he'd dated at all since his divorce. She also wondered if she'd be a complete nut to go out on his boat with him. Somehow she didn't think so. Just the opposite, in fact, not that she was looking for a relationship, because she wasn't. Still, how many really nice guys came along? Darn few in her present circumstances. And a swim did sound lovely.

"Why not?" she finally said.

Reece grinned, but then he looked again to Walt, who was standing now and staring at them. "You're sure it's not a problem?"

She glanced in Walt's direction, rolled her eyes and said smartly, "I told you, Walt's not my boyfriend."

"And you're sure Walt knows that?"

"We're friends," she said pointedly, "nothing more."

He turned a considering look on her. Finally he smiled. "Okay, then, what are we waiting for?"

She couldn't help smiling. "Well, for one thing, I have to go up and change into my suit."

"Oh, right."

"Want to come up?" she asked uncertainly, thinking of Sharon, who would undoubtedly be stirring by now, along with her overnight guest. He seemed to sense her discomfort and shook his head.

"Naw, I'll just hang around down here in the shade." He pointed to a lawn chair sitting in the shadow of the stairwell.

Relieved, she hurried toward the stairs, calling out, "I won't be long."

"Take your time. No hurry."

She tossed him a smile and quickly began climbing the stairs toward Walt, suddenly excited. The heat already seemed lessened, and she was aware of an odd, pleasurable lightness, a sense of being carefree for the first time in a long while, a sense of awareness that she'd never felt before. She admitted to herself for the first time that she liked Reece Carlyle. She liked him a great deal. As a man.

As she drew near, Walt sat down on the step again and picked up the hair dryer that he was attempting to repair, her hair dryer, the one Sharon had "borrowed." When Amber told him that he didn't have to do that, he shrugged and said, "I see you're with that guy. What's up?"

"Nothing much," she told him brightly, pausing on the step below him. "Going for a swim, that's all."

"With him?" He jerked his head toward Reece, who stuck his hands in his pockets and began strolling toward the chair beneath the stairs.

Amber smiled and leaned close. "He's not a serial killer, I promise."

Walt frowned up at her, squinting. "How do you know?"

"I spent the morning with him. He's perfectly harmless. In fact," she added in a whisper, leaning closer still, "he's really very sweet."

"Hmph," Walt grumbled. "That doesn't mean anything. I don't think you should go."

"Well, it's not up to you, is it?" she replied flippantly,

squeezing past him and continuing to climb the stairs. "Besides, you're the one who's always saying I never have any fun, so I'm having some fun. That's all."

Walt frowned, but he said nothing more. Amber appreciated his concern, but she really was having fun. And she wasn't ready to stop, not yet.

"I'd better get a move on," she said brightly and hurried on her way, pretending that she didn't hear him muttering behind her.

Reece was not at all surprised when he heard heavy footsteps on the stairs above his head and the tall, lanky form of Walt the Taxi Driver appeared only moments later. He decided to be friendly and polite, despite the other man's obvious glower, and also to keep his seat.

"Hello."

"I saw you that day outside the café," the man said, his tone accusing.

Reece looked up at him, keeping his expression carefully bland, his own tone light, his body loose. "Yeah, I saw you, too." He held up a hand. "Name's Reece Carlyle." He was not surprised that his hand was ignored.

"Amber's not in the market."

Cocking his head to one side, Reece let his hand fall lightly to his thigh. "Amber has already told me that the two of you are not a couple."

Walt's hand twitched at his side. "She's still not in the market."

He had suspected, of course, that Walt might not be so certain of their status as Amber seemed to be. Now he was certain. But he really didn't want trouble. "Neither am I," he said flatly.

"I bet you're not," Walt scoffed, "not for a long-term relationship, anyhow. I know what you're after, and I'm telling you, not with Amber."

Reece felt his temper rise. Very casually, he got up and stepped forward, right in the other man's face. "I'm going to let that pass," he said softly, "because I understand that you might have Amber's best interests at heart, but you should realize that you insult both me and the lady with your insinuations."

"I ain't insinuating nothing!" Walt exclaimed, backing up several steps. "I'm just telling you to stay away from Amber!"

Reece brought his hands to his hips, already in possession of all the information he needed. If Amber herself had not previously reassured him, Walt's backing away had. No bluster could cover the obvious. Any man who owned both the need and the right to stand his ground did so. "I'm sorry, Walt," he said, letting the other man know by using his name that he and Amber had talked about this, "I can't do that, and I doubt very much that Amber would appreciate you making demands."

A guilty flush burned across Walt's thin cheeks. Embarrassment and anger had him surging forward again. "You listen here, I'm warning you to stay away from Amber!"

Reece calmly stood his ground, though he found himself, much to his surprise, wanting to put a fist in the other man's face. "Or what?" Reece demanded. "You want to fight me? Fine. But don't expect to walk away with all your teeth!"

The next instant Walt grabbed his shirtfront with both hands. Reece swept his own hands up and out, easily breaking the other man's grasp. Walt danced back, fists up, bobbing and weaving. Suddenly Reece wanted nothing more than to reshape the idiot's head, but first they were going to get a few things straight.

"Okay, hotshot, but this won't change anything," he said, raising his own fists. "Amber's leaving here, whether

I break your nose or not." Some of the fight seemed to go out of Walt at that, and Reece realized that the other man already understood the situation but wanted desperately to deny it. He pressed the point. "She told me about her plans. She's worked hard to reach a goal, and she won't back down now. She's going to make something of her life, and nothing's going to stop her." Walt's fists drooped. Just then a door slammed overhead. Walt glanced upward guiltily, and the next instant he was wiping his hands on the seat of his pants. Reece relaxed his combative stance. Footsteps pounded on the stairs.

Walt lunged forward on one foot and hissed, "You better not hurt her!"

"Never," Reece promised just as Amber rounded the bottom of the stairs. Walt glared at Reece, but he put on a smile for Amber, turning to her with a fluid, rubbery movement that emphasized his height and slenderness.

"Ready?" Reece asked before Amber had a chance to say anything. She split a look between them, but then she smiled and nodded, hugging a rolled beach towel against her chest. The shiny purple straps of her swimsuit were visible within the neckline of her pale yellow T-shirt, which was as long as many dresses. On her feet she wore yellow jellies, the clear plastic shoes that his daughter sometimes preferred. Reece walked past Walt and took her by the arm, turning her toward the sidewalk.

"See you later," she said to Walt, rather too brightly for Reece's taste.

They'd taken no more than three steps before Walt called out to her, "Hey, Amber!"

She stopped instantly and turned back. "Yes?"

Walt scuffed one toe across the grass. "Uh, the hair dryer's fixed."

Amber smiled and pulled away from Reece. Hurrying forward, she went up on tiptoe and laid a hand on Walt's shoulder. Obediently, he bent down, and she kissed him lightly on the cheek. "Thank you, Walt. That was so sweet of you."

He flashed a look at Reece as Amber hurried back to his side. She didn't see the way the tall man's face fell when she slipped her arm through Reece's, but Reece couldn't deny that he felt rather smug as they walked away together. He told himself that it wasn't what it seemed. He was not in competition with another man for a woman's favor. Those days were behind him, long behind him. The woman on his arm was not a prize in a testosterone contest. She wasn't even a woman, really, just a girl. But that didn't prevent him from feeling, for the first time in a long while, very much a man. Disturbed, he dropped his arm and put some distance between them, guilt and uncertainty quickly replacing the sense of pride and pleasure.

They walked as rapidly as the heat would allow. Reece remained amazed by the heat. The air felt too heavy to breathe, a warm mist that was only marginally easier to inhale than soggy cotton. The summertime heat in Texas was vicious, yes, and Houston suffered from the humidity that crept inland from the Gulf, but a man would have to develop gills if he stayed down here in the Keys for long. The cloud bank building on the western horizon offered no actual respite from the sun that sizzled overhead, and yet, as they drew nearer the wharf, he found himself walking faster and faster, absurdly anxious to be out on the water. With her. The realization chilled him as nothing else could.

The skiff was exactly where he'd left it. She hopped down into it nimbly and easily, without the least assistance from him, and made her way to a seat. He joined her, cast off, triggered the trolling motor and backed them out of the narrow space. Slowly and carefully, he maneuvered through the crowded, busy harbor. Amber leaned back, her upper body weight balanced on the heels of her hands planted firmly on the plank seat, her legs stretched out before her and crossed at the ankles. By simply dropping his hand to his side, he could stroke her slender calf. The impulse shocked him, and he turned his face resolutely forward.

"You're right," she said. "It's cooler already."

He nodded, as uncomfortable suddenly as a boy on his first date. Ludicrous analogy! She was a girl, little more than a child. Robert Presley's child. He was beginning to regret the impulsive decision to invite her back to the boat for a swim. What had he been thinking? He made an honest mental investigation and to his horror realized that his motive had been nothing more than prolonging his time with her. He simply hadn't wanted to part company with her. That could not, must not, he told himself firmly, be a personal decision. It wasn't anything, ah, romantic. He had merely meant to discover a little more about her situation for the sake of her parents, to bolster her decision to leave the islands, perhaps even to convince her to go home to Dallas. That was it. That was all it could be. She was a girl, little more than a child. Perhaps if he repeated that sentence over and over in his mind, made it his litany, he could stop wondering what that big shirt covered so well.

They drew near his boat, and the wondering came to an abrupt end. As he expertly maneuvered the skiff to a mooring at the end of the ladder and clamped a short, nylon line to the buoy bobbing beside it, Amber simply stood in the boat and pulled the shirt off over her head, revealing an hourglass figure lovingly molded by a one-piece purple bathing suit with a deep V-neckline. Rolling the shirt inside the towel, she tucked both beneath one arm and leapt agilely to the ladder. He sat with his mouth open, watching her climb the ladder, pause to toss her bundle over the side and climb on.

She was small but shapely, magnificently shapely, with ripe, full curves. Her legs seemed absurdly long, but that had to be the angle. She wasn't even five feet tall! Her bottom at the top of those absurdly long legs was round and full and firm. Then her waist nipped in, impossibly narrow, so narrow that he had little doubt he could span it with his two hands. Her rib cage flared above it, supporting a pair of high, ample breasts. More than ample breasts, magnificent breasts. Perfect breasts.

He couldn't breathe, not because his lungs were stuffed with cotton but because they simply wouldn't work. His heart had stopped. His muscles were frozen. The only things that seemed to function were his eyes and his brain. His eyes watched her disappear over the side of the boat, his boat, and his brain screamed at him. Not a child! Not even a little. All woman, fully formed, ripe, luscious. The daughter of Robert Presley, his friend. That put the air back in his lungs and started his heart again.

All right, she wasn't a child, but she was the daughter of his friend, a very good friend, one of his best friends, maybe his very best friend. A friend who was a concerned, conscientious father, like himself. The young daughter, even the young *adult* daughter, of such a good friend was clearly off-limits, especially since he was on a mission here to convince her to return home. Yes, that was certainly his mission now. Perhaps in the beginning he had meant only to check up on her for her father, his very dear friend, but now that he knew how unhappy she was here on the island, he realized that he had a duty, a mandate, to convince her to leave as quickly as possible. And go home. Where she would be safe from the likes of him. And Walt. And every other man who might guess what she hid beneath those simple, shapeless clothes she usually wore. His hands were shaking when he finally heaved himself aboard the cabin cruiser.

She stood in the center of the small aft deck, peering through the long, low window beneath the pilothouse into what he thought of as his living room with its polished teak paneling, deep blue carpet and built-in yellow gold furnishings. The sofa unfolded into a full-size bed, the foot of which rested on the chest-type coffee table bolted to the center of the floor. A television was hidden behind a pair of bookcase doors on the opposite wall. A pair of barrel-shaped chairs and a desk bolted beneath the window through which she peered completed the furnishings. A narrow bar with four stools beneath it separated the living area from the tiny but efficient galley. A small door opened off the galley at the end of the bar into the only bedroom and a full bath. Beyond that was a small storage area, fully stocked with emergency gear, fuel, some groceries and cleaning supplies. In addition to providing access to the powerful inboard motor, the aft storage, which was beneath their feet, held tools and more fuel and more emergency gear, including an inflatable raft, a third radio and enough sail to outfit two boats this size.

"Make yourself at home," Reece said, gesturing toward the pilothouse. "I'll get us under way."

She dropped her things to the deck and put her hands to her hips, turning to face him. Those perfect, magnificent breasts thrust forward challengingly. "Can I help?"

"Uh." His tongue felt too thick to manage, but he finally got it wrapped around a real word. "Drink." That seemed to loosen it up sufficiently. "You could get us each a cold drink from the galley. Just go through the salon."

"Sure." She flashed him a smile and whirled away. She climbed the three steps up into the pilothouse and disappeared down the hatch at the other end of it, while he turned toward the anchor winch. The anchor was raised and the inboard motor humming when she returned to the pilothouse with two bottles of cold, foamy root beer. "It's a beautiful boat,'' she said. "May I watch you take her out?''

"Of course.''

He dropped his root beer into a rubber holder and began easing the boat away from the buoy and skiff, while she glanced about, hummed approval, smiled and took a seat at the tiny chart table across the narrow pilothouse from the helm station, which sat starboard.

Reece put out a general radio call, letting anyone in his path know that he was underway, then fixed his attention on piloting his boat out of the harbor. The instant they cleared the mouth, Amber spoke up.

"Could we take her out for a bit, hoist the sail?'' Her voice trembled with excitement and delight. He smiled, catching fire inside.

"Absolutely.'' He pointed his bow toward open sea. "Have you sailed before?''

"Yes, but not on anything like this.'' She ran a hand across the leather upholstered box, and Reece thought he'd choke on a knot of lust so fierce that it frightened him.

He slid out of the captain's seat and indicated the wheel with a nod of his head. "Come here.'' She slipped eagerly into the space he'd just vacated. He tapped a dial, reaching around her to do so. His hands were trembling again. "Keep her on this heading until I come back. I'm going to lift the sails.'' She nodded and wrapped her tiny hands around the wheel.

He needn't have left her at the wheel. He could have fixed the autopilot or even shut off the engine entirely, but he wanted, needed, her out of his way. He had to clear his head somehow, figure out what he was going to say to her. He scrambled up onto the side deck and made his way forward where he unclipped everything and started the process, turning on the electric motor that would hoist the roller furling sails. Backing off, he stood with hands on hips and watched the sail fully deploy. As the ropes taut-ened and the sails billowed, he locked the winch and hur-ried back to the pilothouse, exulting as the boat picked up speed.

She had opened the casement, letting the heavy glass down inside the bulkhead, so the wind could blow through her hair, which she had freed from its rubber band. She sat the edge of the seat with her feet planted wide apart on the deck, her hands on the wheel, hair streaming out behind her. She was almost laughing, her smile was so broad, as the deck bucked beneath them. He remembered how his ex had hated the damage that the elements would do to her expertly styled hair and makeup. An indifferent sailor at best, Joyce had preferred her water chlorinated. Amber seemed to exult in the sun and the sea and the salt breeze. With one hand, he took the wheel while she slipped by him. Positioning himself, he let the wind take them. The boat practically lifted out of the water.

"It's amazing!" she cried, laughter lifting her voice, lighting her face. He felt as if he'd been punched in the gut. His head felt as if it might fall off his shoulders, which seemed ludicrously appropriate considering that Rob would undoubtedly decapitate him if he seduced his good friend's daughter, his much too young daughter even if she was fully grown and lush enough to tempt a monk old enough to be her...much older brother.

She scampered down onto the aft deck, throwing out her arms and twirling in an expression of complete abandon. He gripped the wheel tightly, trained his gaze forward and began a desperate litany inside his head.

Too young. My friend's daughter. Too young. My friend's daughter. Too young. My friend's daughter.

An absolutely luscious woman.

He closed his eyes, deeply aware that he was in big trouble.

Chapter Five

They turned around much too soon for Amber's taste, but it was his boat, and she wasn't the sort of guest to insist upon having her way. She loved the feeling of flying across the water, the sails puffed out and snapping overhead. It was the most carefree feeling she'd had in a very long time. She got up from the foredeck and gingerly made her way back to the pilothouse.

"Ready to swim?" he asked, not even looking at her. "I thought we'd drop anchor just over there, well off the reef," he said, pointing straight ahead. "That all right with you?"

"Great."

"There's a CD deck and intercom system below," he told her. "It's in the cabinet behind the bookcase. Why don't you go down and put on some music?"

"Okay. Any requests?"

He shrugged. "Please yourself. It's a pretty varied collection. Lot of my daughter's favorites in there."

"I'll take a look."

She went below to the salon. The bookcase parted with a mere touch, revealing a wide array of video and audio equipment, as well as several rows of videotapes and CDs. The music was on the bottom, so she sat down to take a brief survey. Along the way, her eyes snagged on several movie titles among his collection. Apparently their tastes ran along the same line, when it came to movies, anyway. The CDs were another matter.

Most of the first row were what she referred to as "teeny bopper junk," heavily choreographed guy groups, silly girl groups, the occasional gushy warbler who tried to cover a lack of experience and feeling with vocal gymnastics. She dismissed them out of hand and went on to the movie soundtracks, a smattering of classical, and an impressive collection of show tunes. She found some country, some pop, and then just what she was looking for, good old classical rock. Choosing two recent reissues that she'd been wanting herself, she loaded the changer and spent a few moments figuring out the system, then pressed the buttons and stepped back as music filled the room.

She could feel the boat slowing. Overhead, the sails were being lowered. She decided to see if she could help out. Moving quickly, she reached the foredeck just as Reece began buttoning down the unfurled sails. Amazingly, the music sounded great even out here, although she couldn't determine where the speakers were hidden. She hurried to help him, uncertain just what to do but following his lead. He shot her a surprised look, smiled and said, "Good choice. One of my favorites."

"Mine, too."

He glanced up from securing the joists to the deck. "Really? I'd have thought your taste would run more to, oh, I don't know, what do they call that stuff? Techno?" She made a gagging sound, and he laughed. "You really like the classic rock?"

"I've had to talk myself out of that album two or three times already," she told him.

He studied her for a moment, pausing in his work. "Is money so tight then?"

She wrinkled her nose. "It's me. I can't help thinking that every penny I spend is one less penny I can use to get off this island."

He straightened. "If you want to leave here so badly, why don't you just go home?"

It was territory they'd covered before, but she answered him anyway. "Because that would be trading one type of prison for another. It would be worse, actually. It would be going backward, like trading an ankle monitor for bricks and bars."

"That analogy's a little harsh, isn't it?"

"No."

He stared at her, shook his head and bent to work once more. The sail was quickly secured, then he went below to change into his swimsuit while she moved aft and waited for him, lounging on the U-shaped cushioned bench that lined the deck. He emerged wearing a navy, boxer-type suit, a matching towel slung around his neck. The towel did little to hide the hard, sculpted musculature of his upper body. She felt a decided hitch in her breath at the sight of all that smooth, bronze skin. It was almost embarrassing, the way this view of him affected her. She cleared her throat and sprang to her feet. Rushing to the side, she peered over.

"Doesn't look too deep here."

He whipped off the towel and tossed it aside. "I should've asked this before, but I assumed, since you live on an island, that you do know how to swim."

"Like a fish," she said, hopping up onto the bench. She looked down to be sure the way was clear, clasped her hands over her head and dove cleanly over the side.

She had just touched the sandy bottom when his body shot into the water close by. Turning, she crouched against the sand and shoved upward, cleaving the surface. When her head popped up into the air, she found Reece grinning at her, his sun-streaked hair plastered sleekly against his skull. They both laughed. He pointed to the roped buoy several yards away that protected the reef.

"Want to race?"

She turned herself in the water, lifted her hips and surged forward, "You bet!"

"Hey!"

She was a full length ahead of him, by the time he launched after her, but it wasn't enough to make up for his superior height and strength. He was hanging off the buoy when she got there and didn't even have the good grace to be breathing hard.

"Again?"

"No, thanks. I know when I'm outclassed."

He chuckled and slid back into the water. They began easily stroking their way back to the boat, chatting as the waves, movement and breathing allowed.

"You did pretty well out there today," he said.

"Are you saying I have the makings of a real sailor?"

"Absolutely."

"It's a beautiful boat."

"Thanks. I've sure enjoyed it."

"I can see why."

He jackknifed beneath the water and circled around her, their legs briefly tangling. The next instant she felt his hands close around her ankles and had just enough time to fill her lungs before he dragged her under. She popped up again almost instantly, but he was already stroking out of reach. Two could play that game, though. Taking a deep breath, she lifted out of the water, then sank below the surface and calmly, slowly began stalking him. She could see him treading water, turning this way and that, trying to keep track of her movements. She swam right past him, then launched upward, twisted and rose high, shoving him down by the shoulders at the same time. Gurgling with laughter, he came after her, but she filled her lungs and dove deep. Only when she surfaced for more air did he catch her again. They went on that way for some time, frolicking like a pair of dolphins until they were both exhausted.

Never far from the boat, they had merely to circle around to the ladder to climb aboard. Reece went first, then reached back down to help her heave herself out of the water. She came up onto the rung next to him, their bodies bumping together for the first time without the cushioning resistance of water. The flash of heat surprised her so much that she faltered, slipping. He caught her with one arm scooped around her waist, and suddenly she was plastered against him, her breath gone, heart shocked to a standstill. For an instant, his mouth hovered close, his breath mingling with hers. Her eyelids drooped, so strong was the compulsion to kiss him. Then he abruptly turned his head away and dropped his arm. He moved quickly up the ladder and over the side of the boat. Amber followed more slowly, her muscles quivering with more than mere fatigue.

He was toweling himself dry when she finally crawled onto the deck and collapsed against the cushions. "Lunchtime," he announced. Her stomach rumbled in answer, and he chuckled. "I'll take that as agreement. How does a big salad with tuna and pineapple vinaigrette sound? I have some garlic bread to go with it."

She struggled up onto her elbows. "Good grief, he even cooks!"

"He does if he wants to eat," he retorted.

"Guess that means I'd better pitch in," she said, getting to her feet.

He stopped drying himself and frowned at her. "That wasn't what I meant."

She waved that away, moving toward the cabin. "I can take a hint."

"No, really, I wouldn't dream of asking you to—"

She tossed a mischievous grin over one shoulder, and he instantly broke off, bringing his hands to his hips.

"Okay, fine. Just for that, you can put together the salad while I toast the garlic bread, Miss Tease."

She laughed and skipped toward the pilothouse, bending to catch up her towel as she did so. Unrolling it, she tossed aside her T-shirt and sunscreen, kept the small brush and wrapped the towel around her head. He followed her below, then excused himself briefly and returned wearing a tank top over his suit, his thick hair brushed back severely. By the time he returned, Amber had towel-dried her own hair and brushed it out to fan across her shoulders.

He moved into the galley and opened the small refrigerator, extracting the ingredients for his salad. Dishes came down from overhead. Amber climbed up onto a barstool and pulled the colander full of rinsed, dried greens toward her. He slid a bowl across the counter, and she began tearing the greens and placing them inside, humming along with the song on the stereo. After opening a can of tuna packed in olive oil and another of pineapple tidbits, he sliced the garlic bread and popped it into the toaster fixed to the underside of the cabinet, then began making his vinaigrette while she built the salad with the ingredients he provided her, carrot sticks, cherry tomatoes, chopped red cabbage, mandarin orange slices, raisins, and some strips of bell pepper. When the salad was fully assembled, he produced a box of sesame croutons and sprinkled them liberally over the top before serving her a hefty portion and passing her the vinaigrette, along with a slice of fragrant garlic toast.

She was the one to gorge herself this time. The blend of flavors was sublime. The salad was cool and refreshing, with just enough crunch to make it really interesting in the mouth. The garlic toast provided counterpoint. Altogether, it was a truly delicious lunch, accompanied by a bottle of sparkling water with a wedge of lemon in it. And she was so very hungry! She'd worked up quite an appetite in the water, not to mention all that walking. When she'd eaten the very last morsel, she collapsed, groaning, onto the deck in front of the stereo while Reece quickly cleaned up. She knew she ought to help him, but she was just too sated and worn out to get up again.

Drifting in a state of semiconsciousness she listened to the music and the subtle clinks and clunks of a man in the kitchen, the deck gently rocking beneath her. In that moment, she was supremely content, and the thought began to form that she might never be so again. Certainly she would never know another moment like this one after Reece Carlyle had disappeared from her life, which he would undoubtedly do. The only question was, how soon? It was a question she suddenly had to have answered.

He came around the end of the bar then, having rapidly finished with the clean up, and stopped, bringing his hands to his hips. She sat up, folding her legs in at the knees and crossing her ankles in front of her.

"When are you leaving?" she blurted.

"You mean going back to the harbor? We'll have to head back pretty soon, I guess. Why? Do you need to be somewhere?"

"No, I mean, when are you leaving Key West?"

He stared at her a moment, and then he shrugged, moving toward the couch, where he dropped down. "I don't know, really. The only thing important on my agenda is picking up my daughter, but that's not for almost a month yet.''

"You haven't made plans to go anywhere else until then?''

"No. I've been trying not to plan much of anything for awhile. Why do you ask?''

It didn't even occur to her to say anything but the truth. "I was hoping you'd stick around for a while.'' The moment the words were out, the atmosphere changed, became charged somehow, electrified. He was staring at her again. Then he leaned his head back and closed his eyes, linking his hands together over his flat middle. He cleared his throat.

"Yeah, might as well.''

She watched him, relief and hope swirling through her. He looked so relaxed, so peaceful, but she knew that he wasn't. She could feel it, sense that his heartbeat was keeping frantic pace with hers.

"Speaking of leaving the island,'' he said, neither straightening nor looking at her, "when do you think you'll be ready?''

She snorted rather indelicately. "I'm ready now. Unfortunately, it will be a few more months before I have the necessary funds.''

He sat up suddenly and leaned forward, elbows on his knees, his gaze oddly intense. "You've told me why you don't want to go home, but surely if you just asked your parents for the financial help, they would send you the funds.''

She pushed up to her feet. "You don't understand. There would be strings attached, heavy strings. My father would use that to control my life.''

"Surely there's room for compromise,'' he argued. "If my daughter had absented herself from my life for years, I'd do anything to bring her close again.''

"Close is too close where my father is concerned," she told him. "You don't know him. He's such a strong personality, and he can't get past the need to protect me, even from myself. When I'm near him, I start to fold in on myself, to shrivel inside. My life becomes all about *his* life, about pleasing him. I'm too much like my mother in that way. She lives for him, and that's all right for her because she's his wife and she chose to live like that. But I have to make my own life. I've worked too hard for too long to go back to being Daddy's good little girl again, letting him pick my friends and my clothes and my entertainments. Don't you see? I can't let him decide who I am anymore. I can't let him define me as a person. That's my job. That's my right."

He shoved a hand through his hair, which had dried into a series of waves that cloaked his head in multi-colored streaks. The man was simply stunning. "You'd rather give silly tours, wait tables and share a bedroom than go home?" he asked.

"For the next ten years," she confirmed firmly.

He sighed heavily. "I don't suppose you'd consider letting me give you—"

"Certainly not!" she interrupted more stridently than she'd intended.

He grimaced. "Okay. All right. It's none of my business, I know. It's just that I can't help thinking how heartbroken I'd be if I were your father."

"If you were my father," she said wryly, "I wouldn't be having these problems."

He shook his head at that. "You don't know that."

"You're right. The truth is, I can't even conceive of you as my father, but I have to believe that you'd be more reasonable than Rob Presley."

He squinted up at her. "You really can't conceive of me as your father?"

She chuckled. "You really have a hang-up about the age thing, don't you?"

"Yeah, I think I do."

"That's too bad," she said honestly, sitting down on the trunk in front of him. "That's really too bad because you're the first guy I've come across in...well, you may be the first guy I've ever been this comfortable with." Comfortable didn't begin to describe how he made her feel, of course, but she sensed that saying more would just upset him somehow.

He looked at her, then his hand skimmed her cheek lightly, and suddenly he was on his feet. "We'd better head back."

She wanted to beg him to delay just a few minutes longer, but she knew it would seem—was—childish, so she shrugged, accepting the inevitable, and pushed up to a standing position. "Sure. Can I help with the sails this time?"

He shook his head. "We'll motor in."

She flattened her lips in disappointment, then bowed her head, saying lightly, "Okay. Whatever. It's been a great day."

For a moment he said nothing, but then he dropped a hand onto her shoulder. "It's been the best day I've had in a long, long time," he said softly. The next instant, he swivelled past her toward the hatch. A moment later he stepped up into the pilothouse and quickly began getting underway.

She stood where she was, wondering how to name this feeling swelling inside her chest and if he'd meant what he'd said and if he would stay around long enough for her to find out.

"It was bad from the start," he admitted, hands in his pockets as he strolled along beside her while she pushed the bicycle down the sidewalk. He'd changed back into shorts after reclaiming his slip at the harbor, and she once more wore the big T-shirt over her bathing suit. He couldn't remember how they'd come to be talking about his marriage, but after a day of surprises, he wasn't shocked. Something about Amber Rose Presley evoked honesty and openness. How odd that he should be lying to her. He was glad now that he hadn't told her the truth yet. They wouldn't have had this day if he had, but the truth had to come out eventually. Pushing that problem aside, he concentrated on the subject under discussion. "I think I just wanted to be married, you know, and since I was dating Joyce at the time, well, she was the one."

"Wow. A guy who actually wanted to be married."

"It happens more often than you think. I'd say it's a matter of maturity. The infantile ones see marriage as a trap, an end to the fun. The ones who are really grown-up know that family is the only true joy, the only real source of enrichment in life."

"And yet you say the marriage was a mistake."

He sighed. 'Yes, well, having said that it's a matter of maturity, I should also point out that it's not as simple as it sounds. The truth is that we were both young and stupid and we chose poorly."

"How old were you again?"

"Twenty-four."

"Ouch."

He couldn't help teasing her. "Ah, the light begins to dawn."

"Hmm, you made a bad choice at twenty-four, ergo, I am immature. Except that, although I do, indeed, want to be married, I'm smart enough to realize that the time won't be right for it until the right guy comes along, which, in all honesty, may never happen. Therefore, I am working to build a meaningful life for myself, while trusting, hoping, that the right guy will find me at the right time."

They had stopped in the middle of the sidewalk while she delivered this clever and correct set-down in purely pleasant tones. He hung his head.

"I am duly chastised."

"And," she said, wagging a bossy finger under his nose, "you'll stop pinning me with *your* mistakes. That's what all this age difference nonsense is about, you know."

He smiled and looked down at her. This woman was dangerous, truly dangerous. And thrilling. Amazing. "I'll stop pinning you with my mistakes," he pledged smoothly. She lifted an eyebrow, a delicate, dark red-brown, wispily winged eyebrow, and then they both laughed.

"So tell me more about your daughter."

They resumed their walk, and somehow her hand found its way into his, and then they were both pushing the bike and talking, talking. He couldn't remember ever talking so much. By the time they reached her apartment, he figured he'd probably recounted Brittany's first three years in enough detail to bore Amber to tears, despite the fact that she was smiling.

"Brittany sounds great," she told him, pushing her bike beneath the stairwell and bending over to chain it. "I like a girl with enough strength to order her own world. She would never get sucked in like I did, even if you were the same kind of father as mine."

He tried very hard not to stare at her nicely rounded behind—and for the most part succeeded. "Sucked in? What do you mean by that?"

She straightened and turned to face him. "It's hard to describe, really, but my dad has the kind of personality that naturally dominates. It's not anything he does on purpose, I've come to realize that much, but he has a way of making everyone around him want to please him. There was a time when pleasing my father was the entire reason for my existence, and neither one of us could figure out why it didn't make me happy. I can't tell you how hard it was to free myself of that compulsion. I would know what I wanted and that it was perfectly harmless, but when he wanted something else, I felt literally compelled to give in. I was lost, looking for myself and finding him behind every door. I had to get away. I had to. And until he realizes that I can be trusted to make my own decisions and live my own life, I have to stay away. From the sound of it, Brittany will never find herself in this situation. She will never be overwhelmed by anyone else."

He could only stare at her for a long moment, astounded by that insight, one he'd never before considered. "You're absolutely right. Brit's a real handful, but I don't have to worry that she'll ever be led astray by outside influence. She's her own person, through and through. Maybe she doesn't always make the best choices, but she's still a child."

"One who's growing up fast, I'll warrant."

"Not too fast, I don't think." He lifted a hand to the back of his neck. "You may think this is a little weird, but bear with me, because I haven't put this into words before. The truth is that some of Brit's friends are eleven going on twenty-one, you know, ready to be adults and embrace all that means before they're even teenagers. But Brit, though in some ways she's more mature than them, seems to have chosen to be, well, eleven. It's not that she's trying to stay a baby or anything, but she doesn't seem to be trying to rush it, either, and that's always given me a kind of confidence in her. You know what I'm saying?"

Amber nodded. "Sounds to me like you're saying that she's turning into someone you can trust to make her own choices and live her own life."

He felt a little uncomfortable with that, and yet it was true. "Just not quite yet," he qualified.

"She's eleven, not twenty-four," Amber pointed out. "You have a few years to influence her yet. Just don't smother her, not that I think you would. From the sound of it, she's a very lucky little girl. No doubt she'll make mistakes, but you will let her make them and then help her fix them. What you *can't* do is keep her from making them, no matter how hard you try, and you shouldn't try too hard. Take it from me."

Not try too hard to save his little girl from making mistakes? That was asking a lot of a father, and yet, he knew that she was right. Which meant that he had to rethink his "mission." The relationship between Amber and Rob was far from the black-and-white scenario Reece had imagined when Rob had first asked him to check up on his "little girl." She had done a foolish thing, yes, but she'd done it out of desperation, and not only did she recognize that fact, she was now working to fix it, hard and all on her own. Just like the adult that she was.

"You've given me a lot to think about," he said as much to himself as to her.

"Good," she pronounced merrily. "Thinking is good."

He smiled. "Are you always so upbeat?"

"Shouldn't I be?"

"You should, yes." He glanced at the stairs above his head, wondering if Walt was there, waiting for her. He thought about suggesting that he'd like to see the place in hopes that she'd invite him up, but he couldn't quite identify his motive for doing so. Was it to check out the place, put Walt's nose out of joint, or prolong the contact with her? Clearly, he needed to think about this. "Well, I guess I'd better start back."

She nodded. "It's been a truly special day. Thank you again."

He shook his head. "Thank you. I've really enjoyed myself."

"You didn't have to walk me home, you know, but I appreciate it."

"Seemed the gentlemanly thing to do," he muttered, shrugging.

She gestured toward the stairs. "I'd invite you up, but even if we don't, ah, have a lot of time to hang around together, it's not smart to, you know, rush it."

It. Togetherness. The two of them. Him and Amber. He couldn't quite believe what he was hearing, what was happening. He swallowed, then thought to check his watch. Good grief. Five o'clock. "Yeah," he said with a little chuckle, "I think ten, eleven hours is kind of pushing it for a first..." Date? Had he been about to say that? "Time," he finished lamely.

She laughed. "Well, I guess I'll be seeing you around."

Should he finesse this? Confuse things? On the other hand, he, for one, was confused enough already. "Yes," he said firmly. "Definitely. I'll, uh, come around the café. Is that okay?"

She smiled. "That would be fine. I get off at six. At least I'm supposed to. Oh, and on Wednesday, Friday and Saturday nights, I have the tour."

"Right. Okay, then." They stood there a moment longer, while he fought the most incredible impulse to kiss her good-night—as if it were night and they'd really been on a date.

She moved sideways, as if she might slip by him, and he was aware of lifting a hand, of wanting to stall her, to touch her. She muttered something under her breath and slid back in front of him. Somehow, his hand was at her waist, and the next thing he knew, she was going up on tiptoe and sliding her arms around his neck and he was kissing her. And kissing her. He'd have gone on kissing her if she hadn't taken her arms away and sank down to stand flat on her feet. Even then, his lips followed hers instinctively, so that she had to step aside, finally. He was too stunned to do so himself, too moved, too enthralled. She was breathing a little heavily herself. That much he did notice, along with the way her fingertips pressed against her lips as if to hold the kiss in place.

"Goodbye," she said softly from behind her hand, and then she backed away, whirled finally, and disappeared around the end of the stairwell. He hadn't managed to speak or move so much as a muscle. He was still feeling the pressure of her mouth against his, tasting the honeyed moisture of her breath, tingling in his extremities. As if in belated reaction, his heart clutched in his chest.

Slowly, reality set in. He realized what he'd done, what they had done, what was happening between them. Oh, boy. Man, oh, man! Had he lost his mind? She was twenty-four—and incredible! And Rob Presley's daughter! Reece turned around and trudged back to the sidewalk, fighting the urge to grab his head and tear at his hair. Never in his wildest dreams had he figured this would happen. Never. Who would have thought she'd like him this way? Who would have thought he'd like her? What was he going to do now?

He tried to take stock. Nothing had really happened. Oh, he'd realized that she was a woman, a lovely, desirable woman, and he knew that she liked him, really liked him, but what about Rob? He owed her father something, didn't he? And when she found out about it, that would be that.

So maybe he should just tell her.

Except if he did, that would be that.

And why wasn't that a good thing? The immediate answer, and the one he was glad to accept, was that if she refused any further contact with him, he wouldn't be able to help her leave the island, which she obviously wanted desperately to do and which was just as obviously in her best interest. She was not going to take money from her parents or him, and truthfully, he admired that. She wouldn't be who she'd fought so hard to be if she did. So, trying to press funds on her was out. He'd have to think of something else. Moreover, Reece wasn't sure at this point that her living conditions were all that they should be, and he couldn't, in good conscience, go away without ascertaining the truth of that situation.

No, he couldn't tell her the truth, not yet. Neither could he show up at her job tomorrow pretending to be boyfriend material. Unless... He shook his head, shocked at the way his mind was working. He needed a little distance. It wasn't as if he had to haul anchor and sail away in the next few days, after all. He had time. He'd think this thing through and find the proper perspective. He'd figure out what to do, how to help her. And then he'd be on his way. If he worked it right, she might never know that her father had sent him here. She might well remember him fondly in the future, that attractive older gentleman who had shown her how a real man treated a real woman. It didn't have the satisfactory ring to it that he'd imagined it might, but in this case it was probably the best for which he could hope.

Chapter Six

He stayed away for a full two days. Monday wasn't so bad. He visited several of the museums and took himself to dinner at the island's premiere restaurant. That night, he checked out many of the bars, not to drink particularly, but just to get a feel for the nightlife, or so he told himself. He avoided the more questionable places but endured several noisy, crowded joints packed with college-age crowds. He didn't even admit to himself that he'd been looking for Amber until he realized how relieved he was that he hadn't found her. What he had found were a number of outrageously forward girls who'd actually come on to him. He couldn't figure that out, considering the number of young men thronging those places. He took a hard look in the mirror that night, trying to see what those silly girls saw.

For his age, he supposed he was okay. He'd tried to keep himself fit and strong, and he liked his hair now that it had gotten a little longer and gone all streaky from the sun. Before, he'd always found it a rather dull brown and somewhat of a nuisance due to its coarse, wavy texture.

As a consequence, he'd kept it short, which had necessitated frequent visits to the barber. Who'd have thought that essentially ignoring it would be the key to actually learning to like his hair? The sun got a lot of the credit. Unfortunately it was also responsible for the wrinkles at the outer corners of his eyes. Those, he felt, aged him considerably. All in all, though, he supposed his looks were good enough for thirty-eight. That didn't tell him why he'd received so much attention from those girls, though. The sad fact was, he just didn't understand this modern dating scene.

It was true that as soon as his divorce had become common knowledge he'd received some feelers of interest from female business associates, but it had taken him awhile to realize what was happening. He'd supposed at the time that he'd just been unavailable for so long that he'd sort of lost touch. He'd dated quite a bit at that point, but while he'd had business interests in common with those women, he hadn't found much else there. One woman in particular, Marcy, had been quite aggressive, and he'd been seriously flattered, so much so that for about three months he'd wondered if he could be in love. They'd embarked on a steamy affair that had quickly become meaningless sex to him. He'd found the whole experience unsettling and distasteful. When he'd broken it off, she'd told him in no uncertain terms that he was nuts. She'd been offering him—and taking in return—exactly what most men and, according to her now, most women, wanted: sex and companionship without all the commitment stuff. He'd realized then that he still wanted "the commitment stuff," but that he wasn't likely to find it falling in and out of strange beds. That was when he'd decided to take some time on his own.

By Tuesday he was restless but in no mood for sightseeing or touring. He forced himself to poke around some of the more interesting shops and bought a small, antique ship's bell of dubious provenance, which he took back to the boat and hung in the galley. If rung vigorously, it would call someone down from the bridge or foredeck. Once the bell was hung, he tried to settle down to watch a little TV via satellite, but he'd never been one for television to begin with, and daytime TV was simply beyond his endurance. By early afternoon he was literally pacing the aft deck, having failed to interest himself in a book. Finally he went back ashore and suffered the heat while literally wandering the streets of Key West.

He'd told himself after their last meeting that he wouldn't call on Amber again until Thursday, at least, but by her quitting time, he knew he'd go nuts if he had to keep to his own company for two more days. Turning west, he hurried toward the café, hoping that she was as late as usual getting off. The disappointment he felt when he was told that she'd left precisely on time was a glaring warning that he determinedly did not heed. Instead, he struck out for her apartment, so anxious to get to her that when he noticed a taxi approaching, he waved it down.

Moments later, he was standing at the foot of the steps that led to her apartment door. Her bike was secured up beneath the stairwell, bolstering his hope that she was home. He knew a moment of doubt when he paused on the bottom step, one hand on the outer rail. But the desire to see her, to talk to her again, to reconfirm his impressions and assessments overcame all. He climbed those stairs with a smile on his face. He was still smiling when he knocked on the door. A few minutes after that, he was frowning, worried that no one had come to the door, despite the fact that he could hear music being played inside. He pounded harder. A little later, he tried the knob, found it unlocked and opened the door to stick his head inside. The living room was rather dingy but comfortable and quite large, with three doors opening off of it through the wall opposite him. Only the center one was closed. The music seemed to be coming from the room on the left. He looked around, saw no one and called out loudly, "Hello?" Almost immediately he thought he heard movement in the room on the right. "Amber? Anyone?"

The next instant, a woman appeared in the doorway on the right. Her face was swollen and bleary from sleep but nonetheless attractive. Her long, dark hair looked as though it had been stirred with an eggbeater, and it appeared that she had slept in her clothes, a pair of khaki short-shorts and a black, elasticized tank top that looked vaguely familiar. Apparently, he looked familiar to her, too.

"You! How the hell did you find out where I live?"

He actually looked behind him at the empty landing at the top of the stairs. "I beg your pardon? Do I know you?"

"You were at the club last night."

"The club?"

The woman rubbed her eyes with both hands and coughed to clear her throat. "I served you," she said, and snapped her fingers, "uh, bourbon and branch."

It was true that he'd ordered a bourbon with branch water at one of the places he'd gone last night, having grown tired of sipping beer, which wasn't his favorite anyway. He'd been careful at every place he'd been never to order more than a single drink and not to finish it. He thought back over the evening and finally placed her. The short-shorts and skinlike tank comprised a uniform of sorts. "You were tending bar."

"Are you saying you just remembered that?" she asked coyly, lifting both arms over her head and thrusting out her chest provocatively in the guise of a morning stretch, or in this case, an evening stretch.

He didn't know what to say to that, so he changed the subject. "Is Amber home?"

For a moment she just stared at him. Then she dropped her arms and something very like malevolence sparked in her pale blue eyes. "What on earth could you want Amber for?" she asked bluntly.

He hadn't been invited inside, but he walked into the room anyway, closing the door behind him. Conventional politeness seemed beyond this woman. He ignored her question and asked again, "Is she here?"

She flounced across the room and plopped down on the couch. "No. If she were, she'd have turned off the music by now. The system belongs to Walt, and I'm not supposed to use it," she confessed with a sly grin. He watched her curl into the corner of the sofa and don a seductive expression. "You still haven't told me. What does a man like you want with boring, virginal little Amber, hmm?"

So that was it. This woman, who was definitely not a virgin, resented Amber for holding to a higher personal standard. Reece walked over to a lumpy-looking armchair and sat down. "Amber happens to be a friend of mine," he said casually. "And who, may I ask, are you?"

"I'm Sharon," she answered, still giving him that suggestive smile. "And you are? Besides handsome, I mean."

He laughed. He couldn't help it. All the moves, the words, even the tones and expressions were so very practiced. "Reece Carlyle."

She was frowning at him now, but she quickly smoothed her expression. "Well, Reece," she purred, leaning forward, far enough forward to give him a good view of her cleavage, "I'd like to be your friend, too."

"Really?" he said, imbuing his voice with great enthusiasm. "Wonderful. Then why don't you tell me everything you know about our Amber? And start with when she might be home."

Amber trudged up the stairs wearily. Why on earth hadn't she taken her bike or accepted a ride from Walt instead of walking to and from work? *Because,* she admitted wryly, *you thought Reece would come. You expected to be with him now.* Silly woman. As the afternoon had drawn on, she'd grown more and more positive that he would walk into the café at any moment. When her replacement had arrived, on time for once, she'd been shocked and deeply disappointed to realize that Reece hadn't shown and obviously wouldn't. He hadn't promised it would be today, of course, but she'd assumed, since he hadn't shown yesterday and she would be busy tomorrow night, that she could count on him coming today. Obviously, she had read him all wrong.

The age thing apparently bothered him even more than she'd realized. Maybe she wouldn't see him again at all. Very likely she'd been much too forward, kissing him like that. He was a true gentleman, after all. It was one of the reasons she found him so compelling. One of the reasons. She wiped the sweat from her forehead and struggled to tamp down her disappointment. The timing wasn't right anyway. She had no business getting involved at this point in her life. Unfortunately, that didn't make her feel any better.

She gained the landing and stopped to catch her breath, not that it did much good. The air felt as though it were boiling this evening. She was as damp as a wrung-out rag and about as energetic. She literally longed for the cool interior of the apartment, even if Sharon was at home. She knew that it had to be Sharon playing the music too loud because Walt's taxi wasn't here and Linda was pulling a double shift. Besides, Sharon was the only one who knew how to pop the lock on Walt's bedroom door and gain access to his stuff. She was also the only one who would do it.

Amber didn't bother getting out her keys as Sharon

never bothered to lock up. Undoubtedly she was still sleeping now, having returned at about dawn this morning from whatever adventure she'd gone on last night. It was Sharon's habit to get up to turn on the music once everyone else had left. She claimed she couldn't sleep when it was too quiet. Confident that her disagreeable roommate was sleeping now, Amber walked into the apartment—and dropped her jaw. Reece sat in the armchair, while Sharon presented him an unimpeded view down the front of her tank. Irritation flashed over Sharon's face, then a sly look took its place.

"Well, here she is now," Sharon announced, straightening. Reece twisted around in his chair, a smile stretching his mouth.

"We were just talking about you," he said.

"That must've been interesting," Amber murmured, looking at Sharon, who lifted her chin. Amber switched her gaze to Reece, who stood and held out a hand to her.

"I went to the café," he said, "but I was too late. You'd just gone. I grabbed a taxi and hurried over here."

"I walked," she said, slipping her hand into his. She was suddenly keenly aware of her disheveled state. "I'm all sweaty."

"You look marvelous."

Sharon nearly strangled on that, but Amber couldn't help smiling. "Thanks. Listen, let me change and we'll get out of here. Okay?" She glanced meaningfully at Sharon, who rolled her eyes.

"Sure, whatever you want," he said. She hurried across the room. He held her hand until he had to let it go. Thrilled, she smiled broadly. Then Sharon cleared her throat, and Amber frowned.

"I'll hurry," she promised, unlocking her door and slipping inside.

She tried to listen for voices but couldn't make out what

was being said. Sharon was doing all the talking, though. Amber would have preferred a quick shower, but with Sharon drooling all over him like that, she wanted to get Reece out of there. Pulling several antibacterial wipes from the container that she kept in her dresser, she quickly stripped down and sponged away the worst of the perspiration, reapplied her deodorant, then ran to the closet. She pulled down a straight, sleeveless sheath with a square neckline. A cotton knit of pale lime green, it was both form-fitting and a little shorter than she normally wore, but she felt the need to look especially attractive tonight. After struggling into the dress, she brushed out her ponytail and twisted her hair up, fixing it in place with a large yellow clip, then dug out her yellow sandals and shoved her feet into them. She quickly creamed her legs and applied a bit of coral lipstick. Her hair was already starting to fall down and she certainly didn't look much like the sophisticate she'd hoped to see, but it would have to do.

She all but burst into the living room. Reece rose immediately to his feet again. His gaze swept over her appreciatively. "Are we gong someplace special?" he asked, looking down at his huaraches, neat olive green safari shorts and loose white shirt, the long sleeves rolled back to expose strong, tanned forearms. "I seem to be underdressed."

"You're fine."

"You're spectacular."

Amber laughed, flushed with delight. "Thanks."

Sharon got up off the couch then and headed for the bathroom. "I guess there's just no accounting for taste, is there?" she tossed behind her.

Reece ducked his head, hiding a smile. Amber sighed and once the woman had quit the room, apologized. "I'm sorry. Sharon's not—"

"You," he interrupted. She blinked at him, and he explained, reaching for her hand and drawing her to him. "She's terribly jealous of you. I suspect she realizes that she can never be what you are."

Amber gaped at him so long he laughed. "She hates me!"

"She hates that you are so good, and I suspect that it irritates her so much she tries to be as bad as she can," he went on softly. "I feel sorry for her."

Amber was still trying to absorb the idea of Sharon being jealous of her. "I haven't always been very nice to her," she admitted reluctantly.

Reece brushed a tendril of hair away from her face. "I suspect she isn't always easy to be nice to. While you, on the other hand..." His hand slid to the back of her neck, and for a moment she thought he might pull her to him and kiss her. Then he dropped his hand and turned toward the door. "Where should we go? Did you have something in mind?"

She shook her head. "I hadn't really thought about it. I'd begun to think you wouldn't come."

"Couldn't stay away if I wanted to," he said softly, opening the door and pulling it wide for her to go through.

It didn't seem nearly as warm outside as it had a few minutes ago, and yet, she felt toasty warm inside. She linked her arm with his as they descended the stairs. "Are you hungry?" he asked.

"I could eat, but I'm not starving. What about you?"

"Definitely not starving. How about if we save dinner for later?"

"Okay. Where to then?"

"Well, it's too hot for coffee," he said, "so how about a cold drink?"

"Sounds good."

"Soft or alcoholic?"

"I don't drink much alcohol."

"Me neither."

"So one shouldn't hurt us," she said, and he smiled.

"True, but let's not go to one of those noisy bars on Duval."

"I know just the place," she said, and they struck off toward the west, turning north at the second corner.

They were in no hurry, and it really was too hot to rush, so they took their time. He told her what he'd seen the day before, and she suggested a few other sights he ought to check out. She described a family who had come into the café that day. The mom was pregnant, and she already had five kids, all adorable little towheads who stood like stair steps, each one a head taller than the other. Unlike a lot of children, they weren't allowed to run wild or play with their food and had exercised excellent manners.

"They were adorable," she said, "and the parents made it look so easy, but six kids! Two or three, yes, but six? I don't think I could manage six."

"So you want two or three children yourself?" he asked.

"Oh, definitely. No offense, but being an only child, I would never want to raise my own kid that way."

"I would've liked to have had more than one," he said, "for Brittany's sake as well as my own, and Joyce and I discussed it a couple times, but it didn't seem wise or fair to bring more children into that situation."

"Well, it's not too late," she said, then quickly changed the subject, afraid he would read more into that statement than he should. "You know what I could really go for? Ice cream."

"Mmm, sounds good. Ice cream first. Alcohol second. I see dinner receding to a distant third."

She laughed and steered him toward Front Street, where she knew of an excellent ice-cream stand as well as a quiet, even sedate by Key West standards, bar. They found a long line at the ice-cream shop, but given the temperature, that was no particular surprise. The ice cream was worth the wait, however. She chose coffee with chocolate chunks and macadamia nuts. He went for pistachio, and they traded off, savoring the diverse flavors from a bench beneath a tree in a small park between the street and the boardwalk. From there, they could hear the music from the club she had in mind, and by the time they'd finished the huge double-dips, darkness had actually fallen and the live band had taken over. They stayed where they were, people-watching and chatting about nothing in particular.

When a wedding party appeared on foot and headed for one of the tiny wedding chapels that fronted the small park, both Amber and Reece watched in open fascination. It was a true Key West wedding. The best man wore a loud tropical shirt, bathing trunks and snorkeling gear, complete with rubber flippers. The maid of honor wore a bikini and flowers in her hair and around her wrist. The bride's gown was strapless and featured a multi-layered organza skirt that had literally been shredded and cut shorter in front than back, much shorter. With this she wore high-topped tennis shoes and a short veil attached to a bunch of feathers. The groom sported a black, swallow-tailed tuxedo jacket over a white pin-tucked shirt and shorts. He wore white socks with his black patent leather dress shoes. Their dozen or so guests were arrayed in a variety of ridiculous costumes, including a black leather ensemble that included a mask.

There were too many of them to cram inside the tiny chapel, so the Justice of the Peace came out onto the sidewalk to do the honors. He looked sedately dressed in blue jeans and T-shirt, but the black silk top hat provided the proper ambiance. The service was short. It might have been shorter but for the interruptions of the guests, most of which were rather crude. Eventually, however, the groom stuck his tongue down the bride's throat, and the deed was done. The revelers carried the lucky couple off toward Duval Street. One of them was waving a tequila bottle in the air, which the groom captured and uncorked.

"Something tells me this is not going to be a conventional wedding night," Amber quipped.

"What would you know of wedding nights, conventional or otherwise?" Reece asked mildly.

Shocked, she turned on the bench to face him. "I'm not an idiot, Reece."

He grimaced. "I know. I'm sorry."

"I freely admit that I'm a virgin," she went on, "but I'm not uninformed." She made a face. "I do live with Sharon, after all."

"I wasn't putting you down," he said earnestly, "but I shouldn't have said it."

"You did it because it helped to remind you how old I am, didn't it? Or should I say how young?"

Sighing, he leaned forward, elbows braced atop his knees. "You're right. You're absolutely right. And it's me, not you. It's just that my divorce, my whole marriage, was traumatic. It wore me down. By the time it was over, I was so tired of it all. I was even tired of myself. I felt...used up."

"Old," she said.

He flattened his mouth into a thin line. "Told you it was me."

She chuckled. "Know what you need? A stiff drink, loud music and a little dancing under the stars."

He grinned. "Yeah? You think that'll do it?"

"Can't hurt."

"I'd rather just take you off this island," he said, and she knew from the expression on his face that he was as shocked by what he'd said as she was.

"Reece?"

He shot up off the bench and stalked a few feet away. "I can't believe I said that." He slapped a hand to the back of his neck, then turned to face her once more. "I mean, I can't believe I said it *that way*." He strode closer again. "Turns out I mean it." She couldn't get her mouth closed, let alone reply. He reached for her hands and drew her up with him. "Listen, I know you won't take money from me—or your parents or anyone, I suspect—but I can at least provide transportation, can't I? The boat's there, after all, and you do want to leave. I've seen that. We could make Houston in a matter of days."

"And after that?" she finally managed to ask.

He blinked at her and seemed to falter. Obviously he hadn't thought that far ahead. "Well, what did you have in mind? I mean, what are you planning to do after you relocate? You, uh, you said something about teaching."

She nodded. "I'd like to teach theater to underprivileged teens," she said. "I know firsthand how it can build confidence and help you uncover inner resources. But that's beside the point, and you know it."

He closed his eyes. "Okay. Okay. I haven't thought about what would come after that," he admitted. Suddenly, he seized her by the upper arms and looked down into her eyes. His own were agonized, puzzled, as if he couldn't explain even to himself why he was doing this. "I only know that when I go, I want to take you with me," he said. "I-I wouldn't expect anything of you, I swear."

"No?" she whispered, her heart beating so hard she could barely speak. "I think I might be very disappointed if that were the case."

He groaned. Cupping her face, he put his forehead to hers. "What are you doing to me?"

"Nothing you aren't doing to me," she answered shakily.

"This is what I want to do," he said. Tilting her face, he covered her mouth with his.

It was nothing like the kiss before. That had been all gratitude and sweetness and welcome. This was deep and hot and needy, and it woke feelings in her that she hadn't known existed. She first grasped his wrists where he held her face, then she slid her arms around his waist, wanting desperately to get closer as he parted her mouth with his and stroked his tongue inside. The sensations were mesmerizing, not just the rough yet silky strength of his tongue or the constantly shifting pressure of his lips. It went far beyond her mouth. Her head spun, and her breasts tightened almost painfully, while she felt a strange, wet heat inside and her muscles seemed to melt with it until she began to fear her knees would buckle.

As if sensing the problem, he wrapped his arms around her, crossing them against the small of her back and drawing her up onto her tiptoes, her body dragging against his. Oddly enough, she felt the friction between her legs, almost as if he'd touched her there. In addition, her heart seemed about to hammer right out of her chest. She closed her fists in the fabric of his shirt and held on. He moaned and gradually broke the kiss, only to press his mouth to hers again and again. Finally, he lifted his head, sucked in a deep, steadying breath and hugged her close to him.

"I can't believe this," he said, his chin atop her head. "I didn't expect this."

"That makes two of us," she mumbled against his shirtfront.

They stood there for a long while, just holding each other, until finally he spoke again. "Will you just think about leaving here with me?"

She closed her eyes. "Yes."

His chest fell as he breathed a deep sigh of relief. "Okay. Okay, then." His hands moved slowly over her back, and he said, "I think I actually need that drink now."

She turned her face up, propping her chin against his chest. "I think I need that dance."

"Deal." He grinned down at her, then pressed a kiss to the center of her forehead. "No, I never expected this," he said, almost to himself. Then, taking her hand in his, he turned toward the sound of the music.

She couldn't believe what was happening between them, what had already happened. She had always believed that love could not be forced, that one couldn't go out and trap it as so many women seemed determined to do. And she was right. Even if this ultimately went nowhere, she had to believe she was right. She laughed, desire giving way to elation. By silent, mutual agreement, they would speak no more of leaving the island together or what they might—or might not—expect of each other. Instead, they were simply going to enjoy themselves because it was enough to know that possibilities existed. More than enough.

They each nursed a single drink for an hour or more, talking about everything under the sun but the subject uppermost in both their minds. He couldn't believe that he'd suggested she leave the island with him, and yet it was the perfect solution for her. What it was for him, he couldn't decide. It felt both dangerous and right. It felt more right as the evening wore on, especially when they danced, not quite beneath the stars but at least in the open air. He didn't much like to dance, actually, except with his daughter on occasion and this night.

He'd known almost as soon as he'd said it, that the idea of taking her with him had been hovering there in the back of his mind most of the day, at least. Yet, he'd shocked himself. He was still stunned, stunned enough to let in thoughts he'd been holding at bay from the moment of that first kiss. No, even before that, from the moment he'd first started wanting to kiss her. It was hard to say now exactly when that had been. Certainly by that moment on the boat ladder when she'd slipped and he'd caught her against him, the thought had been fully formed. He supposed it didn't matter now. He wasn't sure what did, not anymore, and that wasn't like him.

In some ways, he hardly knew himself right now. In another way, he felt as if he'd come home after a long absence, which was patently absurd considering that he'd never been in Key West before or had any intention of lingering overlong. The island had its charms, offbeat and quirky to be sure, but very real. Nevertheless, he'd never be happy here as a permanent resident any more than Amber was. In truth, the feeling of homecoming only came to him when he was with her. Why not take it—her—with him? Why not keep it—her—with him? He felt like a stranger glad to see himself again, totally incongruous, totally unreasonable, totally unpredictable. Happy. And confused. And frightened.

But not tonight. Tonight didn't have room for anything but surprise and delight and carefully banked desire.

They drank. They danced. Afterward they walked, munching on shrimp kabobs, pulling the fat, juicy shellfish, baby onions, mushrooms, scallops and chunks of pineapple and peppers from the thin skewers with their fingers. When the skewers were bare, they dueled, pretending the long, skinny wooden dowels were swords. She poked him in the chest, and he poked her in the arm, and they fenced until his skewer broke. Then they laughed and hugged and ran hand in hand back to her apartment. Not exactly the actions of a mature man. Perhaps the actions of a man younger than he'd realized.

He behaved himself, kissing her good-night very prop-

erly, almost primly, beside the stairwell to her apartment
door. Then she pulled him into the shadows and threw
herself at him, and he was lucky to leave her as he'd found
her. He could not remember when passion had seized him
so strongly, when it had felt so good to touch and be
touched, even in the most innocent of ways. And it wasn't
all innocent. There was a moment when he'd cupped her
breast in his palm, marveling at its weight, that he'd considered, wildly, dragging her back to the boat with him.

She had called a halt, wise girl, laughing nervously and
dancing out of his reach. He started to stalk her, realized
what he was doing and immediately backed off. When, he
wondered, had he ever acted like this? It was an Amber
thing, he decided. Only with Amber. He marveled that it
should be so and didn't want to go away from her, but she
had to work tomorrow and needed her rest. Tomorrow.

"Dinner tomorrow?" he asked. "We never did really
get to it tonight."

She hugged herself. "I have a tour."

He grimaced. "Oh, right."

"Why don't you come for a late lunch?" she suggested.
"I could take my afternoon break with you."

He smiled. "Okay."

"Then we could try dinner on Thursday," she suggested
haltingly.

He smiled. "All right. Excellent."

She beamed at him, and the sight of her there in the
half-light fairly took his breath away. Her glossy chestnut
hair was all but falling down, tendrils of it sticking wetly
to her neck and cheeks, her lips full and rosy from his kiss,
eyes shining, that perfectly respectable dress hugging her
luscious form almost indecently, leaving arms and legs
bare. Her hands and feet were tiny, her face wholesome in
its simple beauty. She made him ache, made him hope.

She scared him half to death, and already he couldn't wait to see her again.

It was only as he walked back toward the harbor alone that he began to wonder how he was going to tell her the truth.

Chapter Seven

Reece came to lunch at the café, and Amber sat with him for an hour, talking and joking about the other ports he'd visited on the Gulf of Mexico. When it was time for her to go back to work, he suggested that he return later that evening to walk her over to the tour office, but she'd already made arrangements with Walt, who had seemed so hurt the day before when she'd refused her usual ride home that she didn't want to cancel on him again so soon. Reece might have mistaken Walt for her boyfriend, but in truth he was like a big brother to her, doing his best to make her life easier. In the truest sense, he was her one real friend on the island, and she wouldn't intentionally hurt him even if he was a little too protective on occasion.

"Why don't we just plan to meet at the apartment tomorrow evening instead?" she proposed. "We could finally have that dinner we never got around to last night."

Reece smiled easily. "Sounds good. Half past six okay?"

"Fine." She wouldn't be unhappy to see him if he

should drop by the café that next afternoon, either, but she didn't suggest it. She'd already been quite uncharacteristically aggressive in this relationship as it was.

Relationship. Even the word still shocked her. She marveled at the sheer luck that had brought Reece Carlyle into her life. And to think that she'd almost sent him packing only a few days ago! That was not to say she was ready to throw caution to the wind. Only under one circumstance could she truly consider leaving the island with him, and it was far too early to be thinking of *that*. But thinking of it she was.

For the very first time she was thinking of a future with a specific man. And that future could be summarized with a single word: marriage. It followed naturally behind the words "love" and "commitment." She had little doubt that she was already falling in love with him. Committing herself to him was another matter, and yet, love could mean nothing else to Amber, and telling herself that it was too soon to be thinking such things did little good. The harder she strove to push those thoughts away, the more quickly they returned to her. Most troubling of all, however, was that for the first time in over two years something, someone, was taking precedence over her plan to leave the island.

Reece got up to go, sliding out of the booth and taking her hand in his. "Guess I'll be off. Have a good afternoon."

"You, too."

He nodded and started away, but then he stopped and turned around to place his hands on the tops of her shoulders. His gaze dropped to her mouth, and she knew that he was thinking about the kisses they'd shared. Remembering the look in his eye the previous night when she'd finally pulled away from him, that almost predatory gleam, thrilled her again straight to her toes, as did the realization that the gentleman in him would always reassert himself in such moments. A tiny bit of encouragement from her, however, might have changed that. The truly shocking part was that she, on occasion, strongly considered encouraging him. As a result of that most unAmberlike propensity, she was constantly reminding herself that the man would likely sail away one day, never to be seen by her again. Between reminders, however, she was having a very good time. He smiled and leaned down to kiss her lightly on the cheek.

"See you tomorrow."

She nodded, her heart in her throat all of a sudden. He squeezed her shoulders gently, then his hands slid away and he left her. She cleared her throat, one hand smoothing the fine hairs beneath her ponytail, and glanced around the dining room. One of her co-workers grinned, waggled her eyebrows meaningfully and made a gesture with her hand, slinging it back and forth limply from the wrist. Amber laughed, knowing exactly what her co-worker meant. Yes, indeed, Reece Carlyle was "hot." She was still feeling the heat of his touch when she turned resolutely back to work.

It took all his willpower to stay away until the next evening. As it was, he arrived at the apartment too early, due to sheer eagerness and having found a taxi much more quickly than he'd expected. Realizing that it was only then time for Amber to be leaving work, he first asked the taxi driver to drive around the block but was informed that would not be possible due to the unusual manner in which taxi rides were regulated on the island. Bemused, Reece asked the driver to return in half an hour, then got out. The heat was positively wilting, and though he frankly dreaded another encounter with Sharon, even her blatant come-ons were not enough to keep him standing outside in slacks. He intended to make this a special evening by taking Amber to a romantic little restaurant he'd stumbled across in his wanderings. It wasn't exactly posh, but he'd been required to make a reservation, so wearing chinos with a crease pressed in the legs and a clean, white lawn shirt had seemed reasonable. He didn't want to ruin the effect by standing outside and sweating through his clothes.

Resignedly, he climbed the stairs and knocked on the door. A young woman whom he didn't recognize answered his summons. She took one look at him and cocked her head, which was long and narrow, like the rest of her.

"Hi."

"Hello. I'm Reece Carlyle. I'm afraid I'm early. I'm supposed to meet Amber here in about fifteen minutes."

Her eyes had grown large as he'd spoken, and now she blatantly looked him up and down as if she'd never seen a man in long pants before. "Oh, wow! She told the truth!"

"I beg your pardon?"

"Sharon told the truth. She said you were a hunk!"

Reece blinked at her, at a loss for words. What sort of reply, after all, did one make to a statement like that? Before he could decide, she grabbed him by the arm and pulled him inside, talking a mile a minute.

"I'm Linda. We share a room. Amber and me, not Sharon and me. Sharon's the one who told me about you, though. Amber just says you're friends, but I know by the way she looks when she says it that it's more than that. She's such a lady. You know? Never kiss-and-tell." The girl, for in truth she was little more than the child he had originally thought Amber to be, giggled then and practically shoved him down on the couch, saying, "Make yourself comfortable." With that she plopped down in the armchair and folded up her long, thin legs, settling in for a comfortable chat by all appearances. "Sharon's getting dressed for work," she informed him, mystifying him yet again.

"Ah. I, um, see."

Sharon's bedroom door opened then, and she swayed out into the living room, hands on her hips. She hadn't yet donned shoes or socks, and her hair had been rolled up and pinned only on one side. "Well, well, well," she purred, "back for more, hmm?"

He lifted both brows, wondering how he should take that, and said, "I'm waiting for Amber."

Sharon shot an amused look at Linda and sauntered closer to the sofa. "You know," she said, perching herself on the arm of the sofa and leaning toward him, "you're wasting your time with her."

"I enjoy spending time with Amber," he told her calmly. "How can that be a waste?"

"Because that's not what you really want, just spending time with someone."

He frowned at her. "How would you know what I want?"

She chuckled throatily. "You're a man, aren't you?"

"A man with time to spare," he pointed out, "time I happily choose to spend with Amber."

"Yeah, well, when you want a real woman, you know where to find me," Sharon said, flashing Linda a smirk. "In fact, after you've 'spent time' with little Amber, why don't you drop by the bar? I'll buy you a drink."

"No, thank you," he said quietly. "I can buy my own drinks."

Something very like hurt flashed across her face, but then her expression shifted and she slid off the arm of the couch to sway toward the bedroom door once more. "I have to get to work," she informed the room, sounding bored. "If you want to waste your time, it's nothing to me." She disappeared inside her own room, and the door closed just a bit more firmly than it might have normally.

Linda cleared her throat, and Reece turned his head to look at her. He felt an odd sadness mingled with wry amusement. The sadness was for Sharon, who so lacked in comparison with Amber. The amusement was directed inward, because not so long ago he might have been tempted to take Sharon up on her invitation just because he could have. He knew now that he would have regretted it. He didn't want what Sharon had to offer.

"Amber would be so-o-o embarrassed," Linda said.

Somehow nothing this girl said quite made clear sense to him. "About?"

"Her," she insisted, pointing at Sharon's door. "The way she acts really gets to Amber."

"Amber has no reason whatsoever for embarrassment," he told Linda. "She's not responsible for anyone's behavior but her own, and that is above reproach."

"Above reproach," Linda echoed thoughtfully. "That means what I said before, doesn't it? That she's a real lady."

"That's exactly what it means."

She tilted her head again, and for the first time he noticed that her bleach blond hair was literally plastered to her skull with some sort of balm or gel. He wondered if she was hoping to appear sophisticated or bald—or if she even knew what she was trying to accomplish.

"You really like Amber, don't you?" she said, making it more statement than question. He meant to reply that he liked Amber very much, but before he got out the first word, Amber burst through the front door, tossing out apologies.

"You're here! I'm so sorry I'm running late again! That Carrie just can't get her act together. I wanted to be changed before you got here this time." He rose to greet her, and she clasped both his hands in hers, exclaiming, "Gosh, you look even better than usual."

He laughed and said, "We have dinner reservations at seven, and a taxi is coming in less than a quarter-hour. Shall I go down and tell him to wait?"

"He won't!" she said, hurrying away. "Just let me change. Reservations. Oh, my." She flashed him a broad smile and disappeared inside her room.

Reece followed her with his gaze, aware that he was grinning like an idiot, but he couldn't suppress the sheer joy that he felt at just seeing her. Like her? He was beginning to believe that it was more than that. He turned to find Walt glaring at him from the doorway.

"Walt," Linda said uncertainly. "Aren't you supposed to be working?"

"Mind your own business," he growled, not even bothering to look at her. Reece did, though, and saw something that surprised him, an expression of sheer longing. The next instant Linda lightly touched her heavily plastered hair and frowned, seeming to shrink in on herself. Reece sighed inwardly, his heart going out to the girl in that moment. "When're you leaving here?" Walt demanded of him suddenly.

"When I'm ready," Reece replied evenly.

Walt folded his arms. "And when you're gone, I'll still be here," he pointed out smugly.

"That's right," Reece retorted, perhaps unwisely, "but Amber won't, because when I go, I'm taking her with me."

Walt looked thunderstruck. "That's not true!" he exclaimed, almost desperately.

"I have every intention of taking her off this island," Reece said firmly but softly, "and I think she'll gladly go with me."

Walt glared at him a moment longer, then he whirled

through the door and whipped out of the room. Linda bolted up out of her chair and ran after him. Reece shook his head and brought his hands to his hips. Why didn't Walt see that he was pining after the wrong woman? Linda was obviously enamored of the taxi driver, and they were of a type, those two, both tall and thin and free-spirited. He supposed it didn't really matter, but he had no desire to make enemies where it wasn't necessary, and it was as obvious to him as the sun at noon that Amber would never return Walt's feelings in the manner Walt apparently wanted.

He sat down again. Linda returned a moment later, rather glum and subdued. Shortly thereafter, Amber appeared in a simple, tailored bright orange dress that outlined her lush figure nicely and set his blood afire in the process. But he was beginning to understand that she could do that in sackcloth. She had wound her ponytail into a demure bun that made his fingers itch to pull it down.

"Ready?" she asked, holding out her hand.

He got up and wrapped his hand around hers, pulling her close to his side. He was more than ready, for anything she might have in mind. He was ready, in fact, to fall in love, something he was only now realizing.

Amber lowered the magazine she was thumbing through and glanced at the dryer where her laundry was tumbling. Beside her, Reece shifted on his hard plastic chair, and his hand drifted absently over the leg she had earlier slung across his knees, his nose buried between the pages of a novel. Her heart turned over in her chest, and once more she marveled at the path her life had taken. She could hardly believe that she was dating this amazing man, if spending every available moment outside of work and sleep with someone could be called simple dating. What had it been now? Almost three weeks. How could it feel both brand-new and as if she'd known this man an eternity?

The buzz of a dryer's timer interrupted her reverie. She glanced at the bank of dryers flanking the back wall of the small coin-operated laundry and saw that the one containing Reece's clothing had stopped. She immediately shifted, thinking that she really ought to get things out and folded before they wrinkled, but then Reece laid his book in her lap, gently pushed her leg aside and rose.

"You stay put. This one's mine."

She nodded, but then she got up and followed him to the wobbly table where he was dumping his things. Heat rose off the articles of clothing in tiny waves, the kind of heat that baked in wrinkles as it dissipated, and just like the man that he was, he started folding the things for which wrinkles mattered least, socks and underwear. Grinning to herself, Amber laid aside their reading material and reached for a pair of safari shorts.

"You don't have to do that," he said, but she slid him a wry glance.

"Maybe I want to."

"I've been doing my own laundry and ironing for a long time now."

"You could do less ironing if you folded differently," she informed him.

"Oh, really?" he asked, sounding interested.

"Um-hm, take these shorts for instance. The big pockets on the legs are what show most, so instead of matching the leg seams and folding them flat as you would for a pair of pants with creases, fold them inward along the back seam, straighten the pockets on either side and you're done." She demonstrated as she spoke, then reached for another pair and repeated the process. "You should fold outer garments first, beginning with those that show the wrinkles most, usually woven fabrics, but don't forget to fold your T-shirts, either. Also, just the way you stack the folded clothing in the basket can make a difference. Put your knits on the bottom. Stack towels, sheets and under-clothing on top of those. Then come the heaviest garments, pants probably, and the button-up shirts and other light-weight woven items on top.''

He stopped to watch her, one hip leaning against the edge of the table, giving her just enough room to lift her arms, and even then, her left arm brushed against his chest. ''And just how did you get so smart about this?'' he asked softly, his tone intimate, his breath warm.

Her grin widened, partly because the question demon-strated that he was still hung up on the age thing, partly because his tone indicated that he was not. ''I would ven-ture to say that I've been doing my own washing and iron-ing a lot longer than you have.''

He lifted an eyebrow and admitted consideringly, ''Probably true.''

''Definitely true,'' she countered. ''I've been doing this since I was about fourteen and complained about the way my mom's housekeeper did my things. That's a full decade of experience, thank you very much.''

''I bow to your superior knowledge,'' he teased, doing just that. Before he fully rose again, his hand somehow found its way to the nape of her neck and his mouth cov-ered hers in a deep, thirsty kiss. She had grown positively addicted to these hot, melting kisses.

Turning her body to his, she slid her arms around his waist, reveling in the strong, familiar feel of him, the weight of his body against hers, that musky male smell of him, the warmth of his skin, the slight drag of the late-day shadow of beard on his jaw and chin. She was shocked by how right it felt to press her body to his, to feel her breasts flatten against his chest and the hard male strength that pulsed against her belly at times like these. He never pressed her for sex, never suggested that she stay the night on his boat, but she knew without doubt that he wanted her, and for the first time in her life, that, too, seemed right.

The buzz of the timer on another dryer, hers, finally broke the kiss, but even knowing that her best cotton blouse lay wrinkling in the heat was not sufficient to pull her quickly from his arms. He wasn't thinking about laundry, either.

"Hey, listen," he said in a voice roughened by desire, "we've eaten in every restaurant in this town. Let's cook in tonight. We can pick up some groceries after we drop off your laundry at your place. What do you think?"

"I think it's my turn to cook for you," she said. She'd have liked to cook for him at the apartment, where she had a real kitchen to work with, but she was in no mood for Sharon's drooling or Walt's glowering, so it would have to be the boat. "We could pick up a main course at the deli counter and heat up some frozen veggies," she suggested.

"Sounds great, but frankly I'd be satisfied eating out of a can with you."

She believed that. She really did. And she agreed wholeheartedly, but she wasn't about to let him settle for so little. "I think we can do better than that," she said, aware that her voice contained a kind of promise she'd never made before, a promise she truly wanted to keep.

They took a so-called motorized trolley, which was in actuality an open-sided bus, back to the apartment. Reece had bought a pass earlier just for times like this. They dropped off her laundry and temporarily left his at the apartment while they walked down to the grocery store. After looking over the offerings of the deli counter, they decided on barbecued brisket, a box of macaroni and cheese, fresh broccoli and frozen green beans. Amber picked up a small can of mushrooms and some slivered almonds. They returned to the apartment, retrieved his laundry and caught another trolley to the boardwalk. What should have been a big nuisance, getting his laundry and groceries from the apartment to the boat, turned into a very pleasant experience as the two of them worked in tandem with little conversation required.

Once on the boat, Amber insisted she would take care of dinner while he put away his laundry. He took the time, for reasons he was unwilling to actually consider, to straighten up the bedroom. When he returned to the kitchen, he found Amber wearing a dishtowel tied about her waist, stirring a bubbling pot. Standing at her back, his hands riding lightly at her waist, he peered over her shoulder down into the pot and was surprised to see tiny broccoli florets and pieces of stem cooking with the macaroni. It made sense, actually, macaroni and cheese, broccoli and cheese. Why not put the two together? The microwave dinged, and she looked up at him, laying her head back against his shoulder.

"Want to stir that for me?"

"Sure." He reached for a pot holder and opened the tiny microwave over the stove. He removed the bowl and the plate she'd used to cover it, placed both on the countertop and picked up a spoon resting on a saucer on the counter. When he removed the cover from the bowl, he saw that she'd mixed the mushrooms and nuts with green beans. "Looks good."

"I like to add a little ginger and soy sauce, but that stuff's so expensive to buy on the island I don't try to keep it."

"I have it," he said. Reaching around her to open the small refrigerator under the counter, he removed a small bottle of soy sauce. He kept powdered ginger in the cabinet. She giggled when he reached past her nose to retrieve it, and he knew that she didn't mind him crowding her in the tiny galley any more than he did. Inspired by that thought, he seasoned the beans, tasted them and seasoned them a little more. "Excellent," he mumbled around a full mouth.

"They can't even be done yet," she said.

They weren't, so he covered the bowl again and returned it to the microwave, programming it for another four minutes. That done, he reached down and slid his arms around her waist, as the curve of her neck was looking especially delicious just then. She tilted her head, allowing him unimpeded access to the creamy column of her neck. A moment later, she turned in his arms, lifted her own about his neck and pressed her body against him. As usual, he lost all track of everything but the feel and taste of her. The microwave signaled an end to the programmed cooking time, but he failed to notice that or anything else until Amber jerked away, spinning toward the stove. Only then did he realize that the macaroni was boiling over.

Quickly, he grabbed a wet dishcloth while Amber shut off the burner, then together they mopped up the mess. Thankfully it wasn't anything that a wet cloth and a few paper towels couldn't take care of. When the last towel was tossed into the trash, however, they looked at each other rather sheepishly, then burst out laughing. He kissed her again while the macaroni solidified into a gelatinous mass and the green beans cooled to a rubbery lukewarm.

Eventually they did get the meal together and carried their plates out onto the aft deck to eat beneath the stars with distant music from the harbor-front bars as a backdrop. The food was pretty good despite their best efforts to ruin it.

Sitting on the back bench of the aft deck banquette, Reece polished off his plate, took up a glass of red wine and sighed in satisfaction. A few moments later, Amber set aside her own plate, then curled up beneath his arm at his side, her head on his shoulder. He sipped wine, closed his eyes and let the lovely stuff slide down his throat. He felt Amber's hand on his chest, and it occurred to him that Key West had turned out to be paradise, after all, his own very personal, very private paradise, and he didn't want it to end here. Somehow, he had to convince her to leave here with him.

When he felt her fingertips slide between the buttons of his shirt to stroke his skin beneath, he set the wineglass on his plate and shifted around to cup her face with his hands. "You're beautiful," he said.

She wrinkled her nose. "No, I'm not. My face is too round, and—"

He silenced that nonsense with his mouth, but the importance of convincing her to leave the island with him restrained, barely, his impulse to get lost in another pulse-thrumming kiss. With great effort, he lifted his head and looked down into golden brown eyes that glittered hotly beneath desire-drowsed lids.

"You *are* beautiful," he told her, "inside and out."

She smiled in that millennia-old way of women everywhere and lifted her mouth to his, not to kiss him but to lick along the seam of his lips. She'd started doing that only days ago, and it literally electrified him, knocked every other thought and intention right out of his head, leaving only the need, the raw and aching impulse, to devour her. He was deep into that kiss when his hand found her breast. Beneath her tank top. Which told him how badly he'd lost track of his mind, as well as his hands. An instant later, she stunned him completely by pulling back enough to lift the hem of that top and peel it up and over her head, letting it drop to the banquette beside her. The implications literally boggled the mind. For one long, amazing moment, he couldn't think or speak or do anything but stare, as the semi-sheer cups of her bra hid very little of a great deal. Then she reached behind her for the hook-and-eye closure, and he knew instantly that he could be making love to her within minutes but that he couldn't do that without telling her the truth about why he was here and how they'd met.

A great fear seized him, but he knew he had no other choice. He'd waited too long as it was. He never should have kept it from her. She had to know about his connection to her father, and that he, Reece, finally understood who she was and why she'd had to keep her distance from her parents. She had to know that he would never betray her with anyone for any reason. More than that, she had to know how he felt about her. He reached around her for her hands and brought them together, lifting them to his mouth.

"I have to tell you something," he began, aware that his voice was trembling as badly as his body. "First of all, you have to understand that I never expected this to happen, never in my wildest dreams and certainly not with a woman like you. You could have anyone, you know, any man."

She laughed and pulled her hands free, throwing them about his neck and shoving him back against the padded bench with the weight of her body. "I love you, Reece Carlyle," she exclaimed, and suddenly the entire world exploded with joyous possibilities.

He saw his future in the instant before her mouth came down over his. Oddly, it was the same future he'd envisioned at twenty-four: wife and lover, best friend and mother of his children, family and home. He wrapped his arms around her and held on, joy expanding inside his chest until it felt like it would burst.

He felt her pulling at his shirt, and he was only too happy to help her get it out of the waistband of his shorts, provided he didn't have to let go of her. In the dim, distant reality of another world, he heard clearly decipherable words.

"Hello, the *Merry Haven!*"

He heard the words, but they had no actual meaning for him. They didn't register in that part of the brain that connected them with him.

"Hello, the *Merry Haven!*"

Amber lifted her head, and he reached up automatically to bring her back to him again.

"Hello, the *Merry Haven!* Harbor patrol. Show yourself!"

This time the words actually penetrated. He frowned up at Amber in the second before she slid away and began scrambling with her top.

"Hello, the *Merry Haven!*"

Frowning, wanting, in fact, to rant, he rolled to his feet and popped up, facing the direction of the ladder. "Yeah! What do you want?" He was looking down into a small motorboat with the harbor insignia on the bow, three men standing in the aft well. One wore the cap of the harbor patrol. One wore a ponytail and manned the helm. The third wore the uniform of a Key West policeman. Foreboding hit him like a blow, and he grasped the railing with both hands. "What's wrong?"

It was the policeman who spoke next. "Are you Reece Carlyle?"

"I am. What's this about?"

"Do you have a daughter named Brittany?"

Brittany! His heart dropped to his feet, and he heard Amber gasp beside him just before she pressed against his side. "Is something wrong with my daughter?" His voice was shaking again, this time with stark terror.

"We received a call from the authorities at the Miami airport terminal," the policeman said. "Your daughter's on her way to Key West, and they request that you meet her at the airport.''

"What?" Brittany on her way *here*? He was supposed to pick her up in Houston in less than two weeks. They'd decided that he would fly in to meet her, then they'd fly back to Key West together. Originally he'd intended to sail around to Galveston, but he hadn't wanted to take the time to do that unless Amber was going to take the trip with him. Amber. He hadn't told Brit about Amber yet. She was so upset over the idea of her mom getting engaged to his old buddy, Mike Allen, that he hadn't wanted to add fuel to the fire of her discontent. Better, he'd reasoned, to let her get to know Amber first. Looked like that was about to happen sooner than he'd expected.

"Are you certain about this?" he asked the policeman. "No one told me she was coming."

"Apparently she made the decision to come all on her own," the man said with a slight shake of his head. "I don't know the whole story, but apparently she took off without her mom's permission."

"What?"

"She got as far as Miami before anyone realized what she'd done, and it was decided there to send her on to you."

"But how could she? She's only eleven years old, for pity's sake!"

"So I understand. You'll have to get the details from her, though."

For a moment, Reece couldn't do anything but gape at the policeman. Then he felt Amber giving him a little nudge, and that propelled him into action. Grabbing her by the hand, he automatically felt his pants pockets for his wallet and keys, found them right where they should be, and threw a leg over the ladder. Quickly climbing down into the skiff, he reached up to help Amber do the same, then stepped over into the patrol boat. She followed, placing her hand in his and allowing him to guide her. Dimly, he was aware that she greeted the policeman by name, but it made little impression. She'd lived here for three years. Of course, she knew people. He was much more concerned with the unexpected turns his life kept taking these days. First Amber and the near joy of making her his, and now this. It wasn't that he didn't look forward to seeing his daughter again, but what timing!

"I can't believe this," he muttered as the boat pulled away from the skiff. Brittany. Here. Now.

He clutched Amber's hand in his and tried to convince himself that catastrophe was not hovering just beyond the horizon.

Chapter Eight

"What do you mean, you ran away?" Reece demanded of his daughter incredulously, exasperated by the mulish set of her shoulders. Her arms were folded across her chest, mouth puckered in a pout. With her long blond hair clumped into a messy ponytail, her pink T-shirt stained with spilled soft drink and her blue jeans rumpled, she looked as if she'd been sleeping in her clothes for about a week. The bright red vinyl backpack that she'd slung to the floor at her feet had split along the top seam, spilling out a tiny pocketbook, a CD and a magazine. He sincerely hoped some clean clothing was hidden in there.

"I had to!" she insisted. "You don't know what's happening."

"I know you're here when you're supposed to be in Houston with your mother!" he exclaimed.

"But you said I could come to you."

"I said *I* would come *for* you. You weren't supposed to come by yourself, especially not without your mother's knowledge or consent. Just how did you manage it anyway? How'd you get the airline tickets?"

She shrugged a narrow shoulder negligently. "Off the Internet."

"Off the..." He put a hand to his hair, which he felt like tearing out by the roots suddenly. "That takes a credit card."

"Not if you have an account and you know the password," she sniffed in that superior tone she used when she thought she knew something he didn't.

"But *you* don't have an account," he pointed out. "So whose account did you use?"

"Mike's." She all but sneered the name. "He can't even remember his own password so he leaves a sticky note on the side of the computer." She rolled her eyes in disdain.

Reece sighed and slumped forward. He hadn't known his little girl was capable of such animosity. He'd been hearing the growing bitterness in her voice for weeks now—and had ignored it because he was consumed with Amber. Amber. She'd disappeared discreetly a few moments after they'd arrived at the airport, supposedly to go call a taxi. He knew that wasn't exactly true. The tiny, two-gate airport was just about the only place in town a taxi could be hailed right at the curb. He couldn't think about that now, however. He had to find out what was going on with his daughter first.

"So you used Mike's Internet account—and Mike's credit card because that's what it takes to set up such an account—to buy yourself airfare from Houston to Key West," he clarified. "Then what?"

Looking vaguely uncomfortable now, she shrugged again. "I took a bus to the airport and came here." She didn't quite meet his gaze as she said it, because they both knew it was more involved than that.

"How did you get the ticket? You made the reservation

and paid for it over the Internet, but no ticket agent would deal directly with a minor child. How did you get the ticket?''

Brittany squirmed slightly and mumbled something, which he asked her firmly to repeat. She made a face and said, "I asked some nice old lady to do it."

"And why would she do such a thing?"

Brittany bit her lip then mumbled, "I said my mom had a stomachache because she didn't want me to go off and see my dad and that she had to go to the bathroom real fast and I was afraid I was going to miss my plane and my mom would get in trouble and..." She hunched a shoulder again and whispered, "I maybe cried a little. The lady told the ticket person that she was my grandma and got it for me."

He closed his eyes and pinched the bridge of his nose. Well, she was resourceful, at least, but never before had she shown such adeptness at lying. As with so much else, they would deal with that later. "What happened in Miami?"

"Mom figured it out and called the airline. They were waiting with a couple of goons when I got off the plane, like I'm a crook or something."

"Well, let's see," he said, ticking off the offenses on his fingers. "You stole from Mike."

"Huh?" She seemed genuinely surprised at the notion.

"By using his credit card to purchase airline tickets," he explained, "which also constitutes fraud against the credit card company *and* the airline, not to mention that poor little old lady at the airport. There's probably some law about using the Internet fraudulently, too. Then we come to the matter of *running away*. Juvenile delinquency, I believe it's called in certain places." He leaned close and put his nose to hers. "Such as Texas. And, Brittany, if they should believe *I* put you up to this, I could be charged with interfering with a custody order because your mother is your primary custodian. Are you getting any of this?''

Her sky blue eyes were as big as saucers, and her bottom lip began to quiver. ''Am I in trouble?'' she whispered.

''Big time.''

She gulped. ''Am I going to jail?''

He stared at her until tears filled her eyes, and even though she deserved the same kind of fright she'd given her mother and him, he couldn't bear to see those tears fall. ''No,'' he said succinctly, folding his arms to let her know that he was not going to be easy to mollify.

She bowed her head. ''I'm sorry, Daddy. I just didn't know what else to do.''

He took her hands in his and softened his tone. ''About what, Brit? Why did you do all this? You're not the kind of girl to lie and steal and run away.''

She winced at each of the condemning words, then gasped in a breath and burst into tears. ''I'm sorry! But they're getting married! You have to stop her! You have to!''

He closed his eyes. ''So this is about your mother and Mike. Okay, I knew you weren't thrilled with the situation, but you've known for a couple of months that they're planning to marry.''

''But it's next week!'' she cried. ''They're getting married next week, right before you were supposed to come, before you could stop them!''

This was news but not completely unexpected, at least not to him. He hadn't known they'd set a date, and he certainly hadn't realized that Brittany somehow expected him to put a stop to the wedding. Why would she think he would do that? He stared at her. The agony twisting on her face also twisted inside of him on her behalf. ''Brit, you didn't really think your mom would change her mind about Mike when she saw me again, did you?''

"She can't really want him," she bawled, "when you're so much better!"

"Not to her," he told her softly. "She loves Mike."

"She just thinks that!" Brit insisted. "You could talk her out of it. You could! Just tell her that you want us all to be together again. Tell her that you love her!"

"I don't," he said softly. Horror flashed over her face, then sheer stubbornness set in.

"Why not?"

He sighed and glanced around them at the tiny office that had been made available by airport security for this discussion. "Brit, we've been over this before, and we'll go over it again, but this is not the time or the place," he said. "We'll discuss this later. Have you had dinner?"

"On the plane," she mumbled, angrily dashing away tears with her fingers.

He laid a hand on her shoulder. "I spoke to your mother just before you got here, and she said to tell you that even though she's angry with you right now, she loves you and is relieved you're safe."

Brittany's face crumpled, and she whirled away, folding in on herself, shoulders hunched with the weight of guilt. He could do nothing to take that from her. She was guilty of terrifying her mother and, to a lesser extent, him.

"Let's go home," he said. "We'll decide how to fix all this tomorrow."

"Okay," she replied shakily.

Sliding an arm around her shoulders, he turned her toward the door. Depressing the latch on the sleek metal handle, he opened the door and stepped out into the hallway, his gaze going unerringly to Amber. She stood at the very end of the hall, her back against the wall, arms folded. He had the distinct impression that she'd been watching that door like a hawk, and that thought softened the flash of jealousy he felt at seeing Walt there with her. He'd known, of course, that the only taxi she'd have needed to call would be Walt's and that by doing so she was giving him time and space with his daughter. He appreciated it, but he didn't like it. He led his daughter straight to her.

"Brittany, this is Miss Presley and her friend Mr., uh..."

"Dell," Walt supplied, offering his hand to Brittany.

Brittany glanced up at him, then down again, shaking his hand limply and whispering, "How do you do?"

"Is everything all right?" Amber asked Reece, and he nodded, squeezing Brittany's free hand in his.

Walt slipped away then, muttering, "Excuse me."

Reece immediately relaxed a bit. "It will be," he answered Amber evenly.

Amber smiled slightly and tried to engage Brittany's attention, but Brittany was staring at her toes, and it was probably just as well. Amber looked up at him again, saying softly, "Walt's going to take me home now." Then she addressed herself to his daughter. "I look forward to getting to know you, Brittany."

"Yes, thank you," Brittany mumbled without ever really looking at Amber.

"Not exactly herself at the moment," Reece apologized, stroking a hand over his daughter's golden blond hair.

"I understand," Amber said, and her eyes told him that she truly did. He wanted desperately to kiss her, and he let her know it by dropping his gaze briefly to her mouth. "There's a taxi waiting for you at the curb," she told him. "I'll talk to you soon."

"Yes, soon." He knew she was telling him to take all the time he needed with his daughter, but he wanted her to know that he wouldn't let her languish while he dealt with Brittany. They had started something tonight which he had every intention of finishing. She smiled again and indicated that he should go with a slight jerk of her head.

He looked at her a moment longer, such love swelling inside of him that he wondered briefly if he could just walk away from her, but then Brittany squeezed his hand, and he remembered why he could and would leave Amber to Walt. For the moment. "Thank you," he said. Then he turned Brittany away and guided her into the lobby and toward the exit.

He noticed that Walt was speaking with the policeman who had come to the boat for him, the same man whom Amber had called by name. Danny, he thought it was. He couldn't remember if he'd thanked the man, but after glancing in his direction, the officer turned his back, so Reece assumed that the conversation was about something personal and let it go. He had more important things on his mind, like how to convince his daughter that he and her mother would never again be together in the way she wanted and how to make Amber understand that, though he hadn't told her the whole truth, she was his future— and the love of his life. He didn't doubt that, and he couldn't doubt that she would understand once he explained everything. If she loved him, and he wholeheartedly believed she did, they would surely be planning a future together soon. Meanwhile, he had to deal with his daughter and the grief she was obviously still feeling over the divorce.

Brittany meekly answered his questions as they rode to the wharf in the back of the taxi. She had, indeed, brought a few changes of clothing and her bathing suit. She'd forgotten her toothbrush, but he had a spare on the boat. She hadn't really planned this escapade but had decided on the spur of the moment after angrily refusing to accompany her mother on a shopping trip to buy accessories for the wedding. Mike himself had inadvertently given her the knowledge necessary to book the flight when he'd tried to involve her in helping him plan a honeymoon trip for her mother. Brittany had neatly turned that information against him, poor guy. The one saving grace was that she had told her "blabber-mouth" friend, Stella, what she was doing and where she was going. He shuddered to think what might have happened otherwise, for Joyce had called Stella as soon as she'd realized Brittany was missing. He was satisfied that Brittany had developed some true understanding of the severity of what she had done and canned the severe scolding he'd planned at odd moments over the past hour or more. Tomorrow they would have a long, serious talk.

They arrived at the wharf only to realize that they had no way to get out to the boat, since he'd left the skiff tied up starboard when he'd jumped into the harbor patrol launch. Feeling foolish and irritated, Reece hailed a middle-age couple drinking margaritas on the aft deck of their houseboat, which was moored right next to the boardwalk. He'd spoken to them in passing several times previously, and after he explained the predicament, they offered him a rubber raft and a single paddle. He accepted gratefully and promised to return both that very night. After inflating the raft on the pier, he secured the tow rope and shoved the raft into the water, then helped Brittany down into it. He handed her the oar and her backpack before climbing down to join her.

It took some time and a good deal of effort to get the unwieldy raft out to the boat, which remained moored in the inner harbor next to a pair of numbered buoys. After getting Brittany, her pack and the oar on board, he wrestled the raft up over the transom. He and Amber had abandoned their plates on the aft deck, and before he could begin deflating the raft, he had to gather them and the other utensils and carry them to the galley. After that, he settled Brittany, helping her unpack her few things and stow them.

Then he got out bedding and showed her how to unfold and make up the sofa bed.

Fully deflating the raft was no small job, but he finally got the thing folded into a manageable bundle. Getting it and the oar over the rail was a feat unto itself, but he managed it. Then he only had to row back to the houseboat and return the borrowed items. He was effusive in his thanks but firmly declined a drink and departed as quickly as he was politely able. It was no overstatement to say that he was physically, mentally and emotionally exhausted by the time he got back to the boat, washed up after dinner and finally sat down with his hollow-eyed daughter.

"In spite of everything," he said, gathering her into his arms, "I'm glad you're here."

"Me, too," she whispered, snuggling against him. "I love you, Daddy."

"I love you, too, sweetheart. Now I think we ought to turn in. We'll talk in the morning."

She didn't argue, seemingly as tired as he. After showing her where he kept the extra toothbrush and such things, he poured himself a last glass of wine while she got ready for bed. He couldn't help musing how different this night might have been if Brittany had stayed in Houston just one more day, but perhaps it was best. He didn't want anything or anyone standing between them when he made Amber his, not a lie of omission, not her father and not his daughter, and though he knew a certain impatience with the matter, his head told him that they had the rest of their lives to love each other. If his heart didn't totally agree, it was content to hold the notion close until exhaustion finally overtook him.

"I'm sorry, Daddy," she blurted, eyes once more filling with tears. "I guess I didn't think this through."

Reece pushed his syrupy plate away, having disposed

of the frozen French toast he'd made for breakfast. Brittany had managed about half of hers before broaching the matter that so obviously troubled her. "Baby, I know you're disappointed with the way things have turned out," he began, choosing his words carefully, "and so are your mother and I. When we got married, Brit, we really intended it to be forever, but we were young and not very wise, and we got married for the wrong reason. We thought we were in love, but the truth was that we both just wanted to be married and didn't have anyone else at the time."

"But I know you love each other," she argued. "You're not like Stella's parents. They hate each other! They fight and scream and say ugly things about each other all the time."

"And how does that make Stella feel?" Reece asked pointedly.

Brittany stared at him for a moment, then shoved her plate away, folded her arms atop the bar counter and slumped forward, parking her chin against her stacked hands. "She hates it. She cries every time they get into it, and that's a lot even though they've been divorced a long, long time now."

"Your mom and I love you too much to do that to you, Brit," he pointed out softly. "We work hard at getting along, not because we love each other but so you won't suffer the way Stella does." She looked up at him, then turned her face down, placing her forehead against her hands. "Look, honey," he said, stroking her long, golden hair, "I know you're hurting. I know the separation and divorce haven't been easy for you. It hasn't been easy for any of us, but it's the best we can manage, Brit. We stayed together as long as we did for just one reason—you."

She sat up suddenly, swiping at tears. "You could've stayed together for me awhile longer then!"

"Until you were ready to leave home, you mean." For answer, she glared at him accusingly. "Maybe I could have, Brit," he admitted, "but your mom couldn't. She tried, but there came a time when every day with me was an agony for her. It wasn't easy for me, either. I won't lie to you about that. I wanted out for a very long time before we decided to do it, but we decided, Brit, because it was killing her. Do you really want her to go back to living that way so you can pretend that everything's perfect? She stayed in a marriage that made her unhappy for a very long time for your sake. We both did. Don't you think she, *we,* deserve some happiness now?"

As he had spoken, Brittany's glare had gone from angry to uncertain to sympathetic and finally to guilty. "I guess it's selfish of me to want you to get back together, huh?" she finally muttered.

"Could be," he replied solemnly.

"I just don't understand how Mom can prefer Mike to you," she grumbled.

"I do," he said, obviously shocking her. "Think about it this way for a moment. Forget that I'm your dad and Mike isn't." She blinked at him.

"I can't!"

"Yes, you can. I want you to." She looked at him doubtfully, but then she stared down at the bar counter where they sat, and he knew she was trying to do as he'd asked. "Now think of this. Your mom likes opera, golf, cocktail parties. And so does Mike. I like rock music, boating and barbecues. She likes classical art, classical theater, classical everything."

"And so does Mike," Brittany muttered.

Reece smiled. "I like modern art, stand-up comics, quirky movies. She likes luxury autos and living in the best part of town."

"You like a pickup truck and the country," Brit supplied.

"And Mike likes?"

She wrinkled her nose. "Luxury cars and living in the best part of town."

Reece leaned an elbow against the countertop. "It's not that either of us is wrong, Brittany. It's just that we're different. Your mom and Mike have the same preferences, the same goals, the same outlook on life. Now admit it, if Mike was your father, you wouldn't have any objection to him. He's a nice man, and he loves your mother. That ought to count for something all by itself."

Brittany's eyes glittered, but he could see the understanding behind the tears. "I never thought of it like that," she finally admitted. "But it doesn't seem fair that she should get everything she wants and we—"

"Come on, Brit," he interrupted. "It's not like that, and you know it. What she gets we all get, and that's a chance at happiness. I know you were happy before, but you were the only one who was. You can be happy again, if you'll let yourself. You haven't lost anything, really. She's still your mom, and I'm still your dad, and Mike is apt to make a real nice stepfather. If you look at this right, you gain. We all do."

"Not you," she said with genuine concern. "You're all alone now."

He scoffed at that notion. "I'm not! I still have you. I still have Grandma and Grandpa and Uncle Jason and Uncle Caleb and their families. I still have my friends." He took a deep breath. "And you might as well know this now, Brit. I've met someone special, too, someone I hope to marry. But I haven't asked her yet, so don't let on when you meet her again."

She stared at him for a long time, a myriad of emotions swirling across her face. Something very like defeat finally settled over her, and when she spoke once more, her voice was a barely audible whisper. "Are you in love with her?"

In for a penny, in for a pound, he thought. "Wildly," he answered, aware of the joy throbbing in his voice. "I am wildly in love with her." He laughed because it was a crazy thing to say to his eleven-year-old daughter and because it was absolutely true.

"Is it that Marcy woman you were dating at home?"

"Marcy! No! Why would you think it was her?"

She shrugged. "You were with her a lot before you left."

"It's not Marcy," he said firmly. "No, this is someone else, someone you don't know, even though you did meet her last night."

Brittany frowned over that, and he could see her mentally ruling out the various women she'd encountered the evening before. He knew the instant that the right memory clicked into place. "That girl with the tall, skinny guy?"

"Amber is her name," he told her by way of confirmation, "and she's not a girl. Maybe she doesn't look quite as old as she is, but she's twenty-four, and that's young, but it's not too young."

"Wasn't she with that guy, though?"

Even his eleven-year-old could see that Walt had a proprietary manner with Amber. He pushed the thought and the accompanying irritation away. "Walt was just giving her a ride home so I could concentrate on you."

Brittany stared at him, trying to take it all in, and finally she asked, "Will she like me, do you think?"

He felt a whisper of relief. "She'll love you," he answered, covering her hand with his on top of the counter. "How could she not? And you'll like her if you give her half a chance. Will you? Will you try to like her, Brit, for my sake?"

He watched her struggling to come to terms with this

new facet of her life, and eventually she swallowed and nodded.

"And Mike," he pressed gently. "Give him a chance, baby. Give us all this chance at happiness. Will you do that? For all our sakes."

"I'll try, Daddy," she said in a small, trembling voice.

He slid off his stool and took her into his arms. "Thank you, baby. That's all I ask. It's for the best, sweetie. You'll see. It's best for you, too. A girl needs to see a happy marriage. She needs to experience it secondhand so she can model her own after it when she grows up. Your mom and I weren't able to give you that together, but maybe we can give it to you apart, with other people. If you'll let us."

She nodded against his chest. "It's just that I can't help being a little sad."

"I know, baby. I felt the same way for a long, long time, and maybe I always will a little bit. But, oh, Brit, I have to tell you—it's worth it to find Amber. And I hope your mom feels the same way about Mike."

She sniffed, but then she said in the softest little voice, "I hope so, too."

He smiled and hugged her close, fully aware that she did not herself realize what a breakthrough she'd just had. "Then maybe we better think about getting you back to Houston in time for your mom's wedding," he said carefully.

She closed her fists in the fabric of his shirt, but then she nodded. "Okay. But will you come with me?"

He chuckled. "I think I'd better. Then we'll come back here together, just as planned. How would that be?"

"Fine. What about afterward? Are we still going to have our month?"

"Of course. Why don't we make some plans? Want to do that?"

"Sure." She actually brightened a little, confirming for him what he already knew and she soon would, that everything was going to be just fine.

They called Joyce again, and Brittany had a long conversation with her mother. Tears fell, but after they were spent, the first of many smiles broke through. Reece wanted to speak to Amber, but he knew that this time with his daughter was very important, and he trusted Amber to know that as well. He spent that day and the next with Brittany, making plans and catching up in a way that just can't be done over the telephone. They decided to return to Houston in a few days to give Brittany time to help her mother get ready for the wedding, and he arranged their flight reservations accordingly. That chore out of the way, they set about entertaining themselves.

They watched favorite videos together, played a series of board games and finally took the boat out, having lunch off the reef and swimming in the warm, blue ocean. That second day, they investigated a section of the reef with snorkeling gear, then returned to the boat. Over root beers, Reece suggested an early dinner that evening at the café where Amber worked, and Brittany agreed with only a slight hesitation.

"She knows what I did, doesn't she?" the girl asked, wringing her hands together in the way she'd done for years whenever agitated.

Reece smiled reassuringly. "I think Amber, of all people, will understand. When you get a chance, ask her how she got to Key West, okay?"

Brittany thought about that and nodded, then went to shower and change while he got them back to the harbor. She returned up top in plenty of time to help him drop anchor and button down the boat, then watched a music video while he showered, shaved and dressed in jeans and a tan polo shirt. He made sure that her shoes were comfortable for walking, then they set off for the café, taking the time for her to see a little of Key West on the way. He couldn't help feeling a little nervous now that the moment was drawing nigh for his daughter to meet the woman he loved, but his worries were strictly on Brittany's end of things. He had no doubt that Amber would love Brittany if only Brit would give her a chance. He knew that his daughter meant to try, and for all their sakes, he prayed that she found it less arduous than she imagined. Mostly for his sake, he admitted, for Brittany would always be his daughter but Amber he could still lose. How he could live with such a loss, he couldn't imagine. He couldn't even figure out how he'd managed to live his life thus far without Amber Rose Presley in it. And he didn't want to have to.

Amber saw him as soon as he entered the dining room, escorting his curious daughter toward his now customary booth. Her heart sped up at the mere sight of him, and when she caught his eye, he winked cheekily. She smiled, eager and apprehensive at the same time. Had he told Brittany about her? If so, what had Brittany's reaction been? More to the point, what if Brittany hated her? No father would choose a mere girlfriend over his child, at least no father of Reece's caliber. And she wouldn't have him any other way. Still, she worried. They had found no time to discuss how his daughter might feel about her. She didn't even know why Brittany had made this desperate bid for her father's attention.

They hadn't, in fact, discussed much of anything in detail having to do with the future. Just when she'd decided that she was ready to talk, circumstance had plunged them from one emotional peak to another with no time to so much as draw breath. Sometimes she thought she might have dreamed all that had happened between them. Maybe he didn't feel for her what she felt for him. He hadn't actually said that he loved her, after all. Perhaps she was only hoping that he might have if Harbor Patrol hadn't interrupted at a crucial moment. And perhaps she was worrying for no reason.

Quickly dispensing with her current tasks, she moved to their table at first opportunity. Looking from one to the other of them, she could only wonder how she was supposed to behave around the girl. "Hi," she said as brightly as she could manage. "How are you?"

"Starving," Reece said, his smile broadening every moment, "but otherwise we're fine. Aren't we, Brit?"

The girl nodded shyly, not quite looking at Amber, who got out her order pad and pen, saying, "Well, let's take care of that starving business, shall we? Want to start with drinks and an appetizer? The potato boats are stuffed with crab today, and the shrimp balls are excellent. Or you can have onion rings and deep-fried yam cakes."

Brittany said, "Onion rings," at the same time Reece said, "Potato boats."

Amber laughed. "How about if we substitute potato boats for the yam cakes?"

"Done," Reece said, "and bring my usual orange tea and a cola."

"I'll take care of it right away while you look over the menu," Amber said, jotting it all down. She slid the pad into her apron pocket and began to turn away, but Reece caught her by the wrist.

"Any chance you could join us for a few minutes?"

She immediately felt calmer, her spirits rising incrementally. "I didn't get to take my regular break earlier. I'll insist on it as soon as I turn in your orders."

"Excellent. There's just one more thing then."

"And what's that?"

"This." Suddenly he pulled her to him, almost toppling

her into his lap, and smacked a kiss on her mouth. Stunned, Amber hopped back, then she quickly glanced to Brittany. The girl's eyes were huge. She sat staring at Reece, who sat complacently, a silly grin on his face, then she slapped a hand over her mouth and giggled. Amber found herself doing the same thing. So much for her fears that he might want to tiptoe around the relationship in front of his daughter. "What?" Reece asked innocently. Then he leaned forward and confessed to his daughter, "I can't help it. She does that to me. See what a pickle I'm in?"

"We know who the pickle here is, don't we?" Amber said to Brittany, and the child nodded vigorously. Amber shook a scolding finger at Reece, knowing perfectly well that the smile she couldn't wipe off her face hindered the pretense. "You behave yourself, mister. What's gotten into you anyway?"

He spread his hands. "I'm happy, that's all. I have my two favorite people right here in the same room. What can a man be but happy about that?"

Amber looked at Brittany, and Brittany looked at Amber, then they both grinned, comrades in the chore of making him pay for that little public display. Amber put her hands to her hips, suddenly understanding exactly what he was doing. He'd played himself for the fool and put the two of them on the same side in doing so. "Is he always like this?" she asked Brittany teasingly.

Brittany rolled her eyes and said, deadpan, "No, usually he's worse."

"Ewww," Amber said, looking him over.

"Hey!" Reece exclaimed, and then they all laughed.

Amber winked at Brittany. "I'll bring your cola and onion rings right away." She put a hand to one hip and turned a look over her shoulder at Reece, saying, "You, I gotta think about."

"A lot, I hope," he said loudly as she hurried away.

She didn't stop or look back until she'd turned in the appetizer order. Then she crept to the room divider that hid the drink station from the dining room and carefully peeked around it. Reece and his daughter sat with their heads together, leaning forward over the table and talking animatedly. Hope literally seared Amber's insides, a bright light that burned its way up the back of her throat and singed her nose, bringing tears to her eyes.

For the first time in her life, she knew exactly what she wanted and who. And she was actually beginning to believe that she just might get it all.

Chapter Nine

She took Brittany on the tour with her the next evening, Wednesday. Reece dropped the girl at the café and took himself off, saying that he had something to do and besides he'd already taken the tour. Amber knew that he was just giving her room to find her footing with Brittany. She didn't try to force it, just went about her business with Brittany in tow. It was a little awkward at first, but as Amber began to don her costume, Brittany began to ask questions, and before long they were chatting like magpies.

The group was small and quiet that night, so they finished a few minutes early. When Reece arrived, whistling tunelessly and strolling down the sidewalk with his hands in his pockets, they were sitting on the front steps of the office, giggling about the sweet, white-bunned, little granny in that evening's group who had eaten up every word Amber had uttered as if it were gospel. She had gaily confessed to Amber afterward that she was using her recently departed husband's life insurance money to travel around the country from "haunting to haunting." It seemed a particularly macabre pasttime for a new widow.

"Maybe she's hoping to meet up with his ghost some- where," Brittany said.

"Or dump it," Amber countered, and they both laughed.

"It wasn't that funny when I took the tour," Reece said, coming to a halt in front of them. Brittany popped up and immediately began regaling him with the evening's events, which had been, in truth, quite tame. He nodded and showed every evidence of rapt interest all the while she talked, but he kept flashing Amber pleased, secretive glances. When Brittany finally ran out of steam, he took them each by the hand, and together they ambled down the sidewalk in the general direction of Amber's apart- ment.

They strolled side by side for a while, but Brittany soon became impatient and began running ahead. Reece was careful to keep her in sight and frequently called her back. The night was dark, and the trees overhanging the sidewalk provided deep shadows where some homeless soul often had made his bed.

"I have to thank you," he said to Amber after a few minutes.

"For what exactly?"

He smiled and squeezed her hand. "It's a long list, but in this case, I'm talking about Brit."

"She's a great kid, Reece. You're right to be proud of her. It's obvious that you're a wonderful father, but I can't imagine what you have to thank me for where she's con- cerned."

"A lot of women would have pressed," he said simply. "You haven't, and I thank you for that."

"It's not that I don't want to," she confessed forth- rightly, "but I know you need time with her just now." Before either of them could say more, Brittany turned and came running back toward them.

"There's a guy on the corner," she reported breathlessly. Amber let go of Reece's hand and picked up Brittany's. The girl slid into the slot between them and stayed there until they were well past the long-haired derelict mumbling to himself on the corner. A block or so later beneath a moss-draped tree, they spotted several of the six-toed cats that inhabited the island, a Hemingway legacy. Brittany ran ahead to try to see if they did, indeed, have extra digits. The instant she was out of earshot, Reece spoke again.

"There's so much I need to say to you."

Amber's heartbeat quickened, but she managed to reply smoothly, "I know. We definitely need to talk, but now is not the time."

He sighed, sounding frustrated. "The thing is it may be awhile because—"

"Look, Daddy!" Brittany came skipping back to them again, a sleek black-and-white cat in her arms. They stopped when she reached them. "He came right to me."

"Sweetie, you know better than to pick up a stray cat," Reece scolded gently.

"But he came right to me and meowed."

"Put it down, please."

Brittany immediately bent over and put the cat down. "I want a six-toed cat," she said plaintively.

"You'll have to ask your mother and Mike about that," Reece said easily.

Brittany made a face, but then she turned and hurried back toward the cats, exclaiming, "They're just so cute!"

Amber chuckled, clutched his hand with both of hers and leaned into him. "Now you really should thank me," she teased. "I could have told her how easy it would be to keep a cat on the boat."

He put a finger to her lips, "Shhh!"

She laughed, and he slid an arm around her shoulders. They strolled past the cats and on for several moments before he took a deep breath and said what he'd obviously been trying to say earlier, "I have to leave."

Amber's heart stopped. She was unaware of having done so herself until he turned back to face her. "When?" she asked.

"Tomorrow."

"Oh, no." She closed her eyes, panic swelling up inside her.

"It's only for a while," he said quickly, cupping her face in his hands. "I wouldn't go away permanently without settling things between us. Surely you know that."

She started breathing again, her hand closing around his wrist as if she could hold him there. "I-I think so. It just took me by surprise."

"I know. I'm sorry to spring it on you like this. The thing is, though, Brit's mom is getting married on Sunday. Brittany needs to be there, and she needs me to be there with her."

"Your ex is getting married again?" Amber asked dumbly.

"Didn't I tell you that she was intending to?"

"I...you mentioned it, but I had the impression that it wasn't imminent."

"So did I. Apparently, they decided to do it just before Brittany was to join me so they could take a long honeymoon trip."

"That's why she ran away, isn't it?" Amber deduced in a flash of insight.

"You constantly amaze me," he said. "Yes, that's why she ran. She had it in her head that I could stop it. I had to make her understand that I wouldn't even if I could have, which I could not."

Amber tried to figure out how she felt about that, but her relief was so overwhelming that she couldn't seem to get past it to the emotions beneath. "When will you return?" she finally asked.

"I don't know for certain," he answered honestly. "I'm leaving my boat here, of course, and I've booked a return flight for us a week from today, but don't hold me to that. I have some things to take care of back in Texas, but it shouldn't take long. I'll let you know how to get in touch with me as soon as I know where I'll be staying, and I'll be back here as soon as I can be. You do understand that Brit will be returning with me?"

"Yes, of course."

"When I get back," he said, very earnest now, "you and I are going to have a long, important talk. There are things I need to tell you, things I should have told you before, things I haven't had a chance to tell you. Then I hope we'll talk about the future, *our* future."

Amber lifted her head and looked up at him. It was all she could do to stop the tears as joy bubbled up inside of her. "I look forward to that."

He leaned down far enough to put his forehead to hers. "I've missed you," he whispered. "If Brittany hadn't needed me so these past few days, I never could have stayed away."

"I understand," she told him, "and I feel the same way."

"Daddy, here I come!" He turned just in time to catch the child as she leapt at him from a dead run.

"Whoa!" He swung her up by the waist, then set her on her feet again.

"I'm bored," she complained. "We're supposed to be walking somewhere, aren't we?"

"We certainly are," Amber agreed, taking Brittany's arm and turning her in the right direction.

They walked on; Brittany soon grew tired of the sedate pace and broke free again, flitting about them like a moth around a candle flame, until—much too soon for Amber's taste—they came to the apartment building. They stopped on the sidewalk, and Amber turned to slide a hand across Brittany's shoulder.

"I'm glad I've had a chance to get to know you." She couldn't tell what the girl was thinking, whether she was just being polite or was truly as at ease as she seemed. "Take care, and come back soon."

Brittany nodded. "Thanks for taking me on the ghost tour."

"It was my pleasure."

Reece pointed Brittany toward a lawn chair next to the staircase. "Sweetie, why don't you have a seat over there while I walk Amber to her door?" It wasn't really a question, and Brittany didn't argue, just skipped off to do as asked. Reece steered Amber toward the stairs, and they climbed them side by side, their steps slow and deliberate. On the landing he turned her to face him. He slid his hand beneath her hair, cupping the back of her neck.

"I can't keep her waiting long, but one thing I must say before I go. Whatever happens, please think about leaving here with me. I know it's problematic, but you could share the cabin with Brit. The sofa makes a good bed, and I'll gladly take that. I intend to talk to her about it before we return. We can work out the timetable any way you want. Will you think about it? Seriously."

"All right."

"Good, because I don't intend to leave here again without you."

"That's good to know," she whispered.

He kissed her then, long and deeply. It was a sweet thing, both a parting and a promise, and it left them both trembling and wanting more. Afterward, he simply held her. Finally, he pulled away. "I'll be back just as soon as I can be."

"I'll be waiting."

He smiled at that, then tore away and hurried down the stairs. She clutched the railing and watched him go. Brittany joined him, and they walked out to the sidewalk, waved and walked on swiftly. The shadows had swallowed them completely before Amber found the strength to go inside. She had never felt so happy and so sad at the same time, so like laughing and crying, so hopeful and so bereft.

I am in love, she thought, filled with wonder and awe at the feelings that swirled through her. So much had not been said. No true understanding had been reached, and yet hope beamed inside her like a beacon in a small, dark room. She would count every minute, she knew, until he was with her again.

He called on Friday, explaining that their flight had been delayed leaving Miami, putting them into Houston very late the previous night. He gave her a telephone number, then apologized because he was going to be hard to reach, in and out a good deal. It was apparently decided, after discussion with his ex and her intended husband, that Reece would attend the wedding in an effort to present a united front for Brittany's sake, which meant he had to pull the proper clothing out of storage and pick up an appropriate wedding gift. Then he was going down to Galveston for a quick visit with his older brother. After the wedding on Sunday, his plans were fuzzy. All he seemed able to tell her was that he would be out of pocket a couple days. Amber didn't think much about it. Whatever he had to do, it didn't concern her—or so she thought until she got into Walt's taxi on Monday evening and found Danny Bello in the back seat. He was not wearing his policeman's uniform, but she sensed at once that he was there in at least a semi-professional role.

"What's wrong?" she immediately asked Walt. He

didn't start the car engine just reached across the seat for her hand.

"That's what I wanted to know," he said solemnly, "and that's why I asked Danny to help me look into the Carlyle guy."

"You did *what?*"

"Just listen to what we've found out before you make any judgments," he begged. "It's important stuff, Amber."

She rolled her eyes. Walt had gone beyond acceptable boundaries this time, and she wouldn't quietly accept it. "This is absurd. I cannot believe you went so far as to investigate Reece!"

"I know, but—"

"But nothing! He's a good man, and I'm crazy about him. Do you understand that?"

"He's a friend of your father's!" Walt blurted.

She heard him, but it took a moment for the words to sink in, and even then they failed to make sense. "What are you talking about? That's nonsense. If Reece knew my father, he'd have told me."

"They've been business associates for years," Walt insisted doggedly. "Carlyle's from Texas. He went up to your dad's house in Dallas and spent the night just before he set sail. He came here looking for you, Amber. Think about it. He came here looking for you on your father's behalf."

"You don't have any proof of that," she whispered, but the implications were already rearing their ugly heads. It couldn't be. He'd have told her. Eventually. Suddenly everything he'd said to her that last evening was cast into a whole new light, and it was not the flickering light of romance.

There are things I need to tell you, things I should have told you before... Whatever happens, please think about leaving here with me…because I don't intend to leave here again without you.

What better way to convince her to go with him than to pretend to love her? It had been out of the question in the beginning. The age thing, the fourteen years between them had seemed like such a big deal to him, but she'd kept insisting that it was not. Could he have taken that as a signal that she was interested in him romantically? Of course he had, because that was exactly what it had been. She felt suddenly as if someone had poured ice water through her veins.

No doubt, after convincing her to leave the island with him, he intended to deliver her straight to her father. For her own good. And she had thought he understood. A father as dedicated as Reece would likely go to any extreme to reunite a friend and his daughter. He would even romance her, believing all the while that the ends justified the means. Trembling inside, she twisted around in her seat and stared at Danny Bello. "How did you find out?"

"A colleague of mine in Dallas set us up with someone who could ask around," he said gently. "Carlyle and your father have known each other for five or six years, ever since Carlyle did some consulting for your dad's firm. He definitely spent the night at your parents' home right before he set sail."

Amber turned around. Her mind was racing, quickly and relentlessly culling proof from all Reece had said and done—or hadn't said and done—since she'd known him. They'd talked at length about members of his family, but he'd never so much as asked her to describe her parents. Because obviously he already knew what they were like, what they looked like, how they behaved. He'd argued her father's case quite ably in the beginning. Then he'd stopped that and taken another, more personal, tack.

He had asked her to leave with him. She had balked,

and he had immediately upped the stakes. He had never told her that he loved her, and he'd had at least one opportunity to do so *after* she had told him how she felt. Pain suddenly lanced through her. She covered her face with her hands, hot tears spilling from her eyes. How would he have broken it off with her? The age difference would have played into it; Brittany would almost certainly need his undivided attention. A summer fling, perhaps? What a fool she had been, what a *child*. Dimly, she felt Walt's hand clumsily patting her shoulder, but she twisted away from him and sobbed, consumed by the betrayal, the death of her dreams, too hurt to care who witnessed her humiliation.

Walt dropped off Danny and drove her home. Linda was there. She took one look at Amber and demanded to know what was going on. Walt told her, and the two of them argued about it heatedly, with Walt defending his actions and Linda insisting that he had investigated Reece only because he, Walt, wanted Amber for himself. She was very vocal in her belief that, whatever his reason for coming to the island, Reece obviously cared deeply for Amber. Heartsick, Amber couldn't truly hear her. She left them arguing with each other and went to bed, where she stayed until she could find the strength to go about her business without tears.

Her life, which had seemed so full of promise and hope recently, now hung in a strange limbo. She did her best to ignore her broken heart and go about daily life as usual, but she did it all in an emotional fog from which she desperately did not want to surface. She would not talk about Reece except to say that she didn't want to see or speak to him again. When Sharon delivered the news that Reece had called to say he was returning to the island the next day, Thursday, exactly one week after he'd left, Amber listened without comment and went to her room, where she studiously refused to even think about seeing him again. She was very afraid of what she would do if she did. She was just, suddenly, very afraid, for she was not the person she had believed herself to be, and yet she had no choice but to be who she was—if only she could somehow figure out who that was now.

Reece looked around the small, busy airport lobby and frowned. She wasn't here, and he had been so certain that she would be. Uneasily, he recalled that he hadn't managed to speak to her in days, and when he'd left the last message with Sharon, she'd said tauntingly, "It won't make any difference. She doesn't want to see you." Then she'd simply hung up.

It wasn't true, of course. It couldn't be. Amber loved him. He hoped, believed, they would spend the rest of their lives together. Sharon was just being her usual difficult, envious self.

He went straight to a pay phone and called the apartment again to let Amber know that he and Brittany had arrived. This time it was Linda who answered. When he asked to speak to Amber, Linda informed him regretfully that Amber wouldn't come to the phone. "What on earth is going on?" he demanded, all too aware of Brittany at his side.

"She told me not to talk to you," Linda confessed quietly. "She says she never wants to see you again, but I don't believe she means it. If you want her, though, you're going to have to fight for her."

He started to tell her that he'd already done that once recently and he was more than willing to do so again, but she hung up. He could only stare at the phone, unease bursting into full alarm. What had happened? More importantly, how could he fix it?

Brittany asked those very questions on the taxi ride to the harbor, but he didn't have any answers for her until she asked meekly, "Is it me, Daddy?"

"No, sweetie. No, no. Amber likes you. She told me so."

Brittany frowned thoughtfully at that. "Maybe she likes me, but she doesn't want to be my stepmom. Maybe if I told her I'll be good, it would be all right."

"Sugar, that's not necessary," he said distractedly. "Whatever it is, I promise it's not you." He didn't think. They hadn't really discussed it, he and Amber, but he'd left Key West with the impression that Amber was counting on a future for the two of them as much as he was, and he hadn't had the impression that Brittany represented any problem for her. But what was the problem then? He thought of the raging argument he'd had with her father only two days ago.

They had almost come to blows. Amber was right about Rob's irrational possessiveness when it came to her. He kept referring to her as his baby, his little girl, and he'd accused Reece of "robbing the cradle" and betraying him. At one point he'd tried to throw Reece out of his house. Only the intervention of Amber's mother, Happy, had kept them from knocking each other's lights out. Reece had argued fervently that Rob didn't even know his daughter, that his obsessiveness had driven her away so long ago that he couldn't possibly know the woman she'd become. Rob kept declaring that her "irresponsible actions" eloquently branded her an emotional child if not a legal one. In the end, Reece had simply stated that he was going to marry Amber and that Rob could either face facts and accept her on her terms or he could miss his daughter and his future grandchildren for the rest of his life.

At the mention of grandchildren, Rob had looked like a man who'd been poleaxed. Happy had called Reece's hotel later to say that she, for one, wished him and Amber happiness. She insisted that Rob would come around, that he'd already asked her if he might be a better grandfather than

he had been a father. This was news Reece desperately
wanted to give to Amber. He hoped it might give her hope
for a healthier relationship with her father in the future and
perhaps mitigate his failure to be completely honest with
her.

Could she somehow have learned about his connection
with her father in his absence? It seemed unlikely, but he
couldn't believe that the problem was his daughter. Amber's, or any other woman's, aversion to his daughter
would be the one thing with which he could not deal, but
he couldn't believe that was the problem here. Amber
would tell him straight up if she didn't think she could
handle being Brittany's stepmother. No, it had to be something else, and whatever that might be, he would find a
way to make it right. He had to, because losing Amber
was just not an option with which he could live.

The night passed in agonizing sloth. Words, fears, worries lodged themselves in his head and would not be dis-
placed. He had known it would be so, and had offered
Brittany the bedroom, but she'd insisted that she preferred
to bunk in the outer cabin. He'd assumed that she wanted
quick access to the refrigerator and the sound system and
let her have her way, too tired and worried to argue about
something that didn't really matter.

It was that hour before dawn, that moment of pervasive
stillness, when sleep finally took him. He woke with an
uneasy start to the harsh light of late morning, fully aware,
every sense alert. Still as death, he listened to the gentle
lap of water against the hull, the distant sound of a trolling
motor and even farther out the excited cries of the birds
that the tourists sometimes fed from the wharf, but he
heard nothing that explained the deep sense of apprehen-
sion gripping him. He immediately thought of Amber and
Brittany. One or both of them could be in danger. How he

knew this he neither questioned nor explained. If it was Amber, he had no immediate way of discovering it. Brittany was another matter.

Throwing back the covers, he rocked up to his feet. A T-shirt lay handy on the foot of the bed. He snatched it up as he moved sideways toward the hatch. He stumbled over his shoes in the narrow space, then stepped back and picked them up. Shoes and shirt in hand, clad only in the gym shorts in which he'd slept, he entered the salon. The bed was unfolded, but Brittany was nowhere to be seen. Fighting back real fear, he called her name while jerking on the shirt.

Nothing.

Swiftly, he carried the canvas shoes up into the pilot-house, dropped them and stuffed his feet inside while scanning the area and shouting her name.

Silence.

Terrified now, he looked over the rail—at nothing. The skiff was gone. And Brittany had taken it. But why? Where?

Maybe if I told her I'll be good...

Dear God. She had asked if he'd be seeing Amber this morning, and he had told her that he might go to the café, so that would be the logical place for her to head. If she made it to the wharf. He'd allowed her to handle the skiff before, but never to dock it and never on her own. His heart in his throat, he looked toward the shore, but he couldn't see the skiff even if it was there because it rode so low in the water. It could be capsized between two bigger boats, and no one would know unless they were looking for it. He ran out onto the aft deck and dove cleanly over the side to begin swimming in the direction the skiff would have taken.

Amber strode up the sidewalk, looking neither right nor left. She hadn't ridden in Walt's taxi since the night he'd picked her up with Danny sitting in the back seat. It wasn't fair. He hadn't been the one to lie to her, but the reason why he'd exposed those lies was sufficiently complicated to make her want to keep her distance. She sensed that he was hurt and couldn't care. It was all she could do to go through the daily motions.

She came to the alley next to the café and turned up it, then paused as a figure darted from the front of the building toward her. The girl's long blond hair looked as though it hadn't been combed yet that morning, and her clothing, a sleeveless denim short set, was as rumpled as if she'd slept in it. Amber glanced around, expecting Reece to appear at any moment, her heart suddenly hammering.

"Brittany, what are you doing here? Where's your father?"

The child rocked up onto her tiptoes and began twisting her hands together. "He's not here. I had to see you, and I knew he'd say I shouldn't, but I gotta tell you something."

Amber didn't know if she was more relieved or disappointed. She looked the girl over carefully. Her shoes were wet. "You ran away again, didn't you?"

The girl's face distorted. Her fingers tangled together. "Not really. If I hurry, I can get back before he even knows I'm gone."

"Brittany, you didn't take the skiff, did you?" But of course she had. How else would she have gotten here.

The child was clearly distressed. "I just wanted to talk to you. I didn't mean to do anything wrong."

Amber desperately wanted to turn and walk away, but she couldn't do it, not with Brittany looking ready to burst into tears. Resigned, Amber nodded. "I have to get to work soon, but I can give you a few minutes. Say whatever you need to."

Brittany bit her lip and bowed her head. "You won't believe me now."

"What do you mean?"

Brittany looked up, her face contorted as if in pain. "I wanted to tell you that I won't be bad anymore. I didn't mean to run away this time! I just wanted to tell you that I'll be good. I won't even be living with you most of the time."

Amber could only shake her head. "What are you talking about, honey?"

"I know you're breaking up with my dad because I ran away and broke all those laws and tried to get him back with my mom! But she's married to Mike now, and Daddy doesn't love her, anyway. He loves you!"

The words were both a balm and an agony. Amber closed her eyes briefly and tried to marshal her thoughts. "That's not why I won't see your dad."

"I'll do my best to be good," Brittany promised glumly.

Amber blinked back tears and put her arms around the girl. "Sweetie, it doesn't have anything to do with you. Please don't think that."

"Then why?" she all but wailed. "It has to be me! He's so perfect you can't help but love him."

"Maybe I can't," Amber told her, "but that doesn't excuse what he did." She closed her eyes, shamed by the bitterness that she heard in her own voice. "It's all terribly complicated," she went on more moderately, "but it has nothing at all to do with you. I don't want to criticize your dad to you, but no one's perfect. He's an excellent father, and you owe him every allegiance, but he has only himself to blame for what's happened between us. He didn't tell me the truth about something very important."

Brittany drew her brows together in confusion. "My daddy always tells the truth," she said.

"Not this time," Amber insisted, but then she shook her

head. Brittany did not need to be involved in her problems, no matter what her father had or hadn't done. "Listen to me. Nothing that has happened is in any way your fault. You're not to worry about your father and me. It has nothing to do with you."

"I can't help it," Brittany said in a small voice. "He was so sad and worried last night. He'll be unhappy if you don't make up with him. He told me that he wants to marry you."

That news pierced Amber's heart as sharply as any arrow, but before she could even begin to formulate a reply to it, a movement at the edge of her vision snagged her attention, and she turned her head to see Reece cross the street to stand next to his daughter. He was wet from head to toe, his T-shirt, shorts and canvas shoes drenched. Amber dropped her arms and stepped back as Brittany squeezed her eyes shut, hissing in a breath through her teeth.

"I'm sorry, Daddy. You told me not to say anything until you could ask her."

"Ask her what, Brit?"

"To marry you."

Reece sighed and shoved his hands back over his head, skimming his hair flat. "It's all right. I'm more concerned about this habit of bolting that you've developed lately. You shouldn't be handling the skiff alone. I was terrified when I found you and it gone. I had to swim in from the boat."

"I couldn't help it," Brittany said mulishly. "I had to talk to Amber." She neatly switched tactics then, declaring, "You didn't lie to her. Did you, Daddy?"

He looked at Amber with sad eyes and said, "I'm afraid I did, Brittany."

Hugging herself, Amber looked away, only then realizing how much she had hoped that she was mistaken.

"I didn't tell Amber something that she had every right to know," he went on.

"But, Daddy—"

"I didn't tell her at first because I was afraid she wouldn't talk to me," he interrupted. "I didn't tell her later because I was afraid she'd stop seeing me."

Amber spun away, unwilling to hear more, tears barely held at bay. "I have to get to work." Before she could move away, Reece reached out and clamped a hand down on her forearm. She froze, the contact jolting through her like a bolt of electricity. Her composure was hanging by a thread. He immediately released her, but a moment passed before she could breathe again.

"How did you find out?" he asked.

She answered automatically, as if her responses were programmed. "Walt. He asked a friend on the police force to check you out."

"Danny someone," Reece said, as much to himself as her. "He was the one who came out with the Harbor Patrol."

She nodded, finally recovering herself enough to think. "I have to go in."

"Please let me explain," he pled.

Oh, how she wanted to. But she didn't dare. "I'm late for work."

"Please, Amber."

She was already walking away, heading for the café's front door, her footsteps coming faster and faster. She usually went in the back, but she had to get off the sidewalk immediately before she lost what strength she'd managed to hang on to. She ran up the steps and shoved at the door, relieved beyond words to find it already unlocked. As it closed behind her, she heard him say her name once more, but she shut off the sound of it, pushed away the deep longing that she imagined his voice had held. He had lied to her. He had admitted it. She dared not forgive or forget it. Her independence was at stake, her very self. These tears would surely go away. Right about the same time as this ache in her chest.

Chapter Ten

Water dripped from his shirttail and plopped onto the already sodden toes of his shoes. Reece felt, heard and even smelled it, as the secondary contents of a harbor as crowded as Conch were only somewhat better than the average sewer. None of that mattered, however, as he watched the café door close behind Amber. The depth and wealth of the pain in her eyes had nearly brought him to his knees. He had caused her that pain. He had caused her that pain for his own ease. Telling her the truth would have complicated his life. It was just that basic and that awful. He had to fix it. Somehow, he had to stop the hurting, at least for her. His own pain meant little after looking into her eyes. The question was, how could he do it?

A small hand slid into his, and he instinctively flexed his fingers around it. Looking down, he saw his daughter's sad, upturned face.

"I'm sorry, Daddy."

He nodded and gave her his best smile, not a very heartening effort, apparently. Only belatedly did he think to do his daddy thing, which gave him an excuse to frown again. "If you ever again take off without my express permission, young lady, you'll be grounded until you're old enough to vote." She looked down and nodded glumly, and emotion suddenly swamped him. Blinking back tears, he said softly, "But thanks for trying to help."

She squeezed his hand and looked up again, her big blue eyes full of sympathy. "At least she still loves you, Daddy. Maybe she'll get over being mad."

He felt an immediate lightening of mood, as if the sun had suddenly pulsed brighter, but the next instant it faded. Shaking his head, he said, "I think she did love me, but I pretty much killed that by not telling her the truth when I had the chance."

"No," Brittany said stubbornly, "she still loves you. She said so."

There was that sunburst again, a little brighter this time. "When?"

"Just now, a minute ago."

He studied her expression. "What was said exactly?"

Brittany screwed up her face, trying to remember definite words. "Well, first I said something like she couldn't help loving you because nobody can—except Mom, I guess, but I didn't think of that."

"What did Amber say?" Reece prodded impatiently.

Brittany's face relaxed, indicating that she was quite certain about this part. "What Amber said," Brittany reported, "is that maybe she couldn't help loving you but that didn't make up for how you lied to her. Something like that."

Disappointment mingled with longing. It wasn't exactly a fervent exclamation of devotion, but it was reason for cautious hope. Perhaps, if she still loved him even a little, just a fraction as much as he loved her, they could work through this, provided he could convince her to listen to him, to forgive. He had to make her understand why he'd done it and that he would never do anything so stupid again. Somehow, he had to make her listen. A possibility entered his mind. It would mean convincing someone else to help him, and that could be difficult, but he had nothing to lose by trying.

He began to plan the steps. The first thing to do was to clean up and make himself presentable, which meant returning to the boat. Then he had to find Linda. He was pretty sure that she worked first shift from Saturday through Wednesday, which was how Amber managed to get the weekends off. Maybe he'd get lucky and find her at the apartment. If not, he'd have to look for her. It promised to be a busy day. Clutching Brittany's hand, he turned and headed back toward the wharf, his mind too busy to notice the uncomfortable, irritating squish of his shoes.

Amber looked up the flight of stairs and sighed. It had never seemed so very tall before. Each step looked like a mountain, a product, no doubt, of her extreme exhaustion. She knew that it was an exhaustion born of emotion rather than exertion because the café had been no more busy today than usual and she hadn't even walked home after work. When Walt had dropped by at the end of her shift to once more offer her a ride, she had taken him up on it for fear that Reece or Brittany or both might lay in wait around some corner on the way here. That was the real source of her fatigue. Seeing first Brittany and then Reece that morning had proven even more difficult than she had imagined. They both had seemed so sad, and Amber was exhausted from not thinking about it. How many times must one reject a thought before it ceased to occur?

"Ready to go up?" Walt asked. He had been extremely solicitous since he'd revealed the truth that had destroyed her world. She couldn't be comfortable with it, but neither could she exert herself to set him straight.

"Shouldn't you get back to work?" she asked, beginning to climb.

"I can take a few minutes," he answered lightly. She sighed inwardly and kept going, Walt coming up behind her. Step after step after step, she made her way to the landing and then to the door. Since Linda was supposed to be home, she didn't bother getting out her keys. The knob turned beneath her hand, and the door swung open, just as expected. She stepped into the living room, paused to let the air-conditioning caress her heated skin, then automatically glanced around.

Reece stood in front of the sofa, his hands in the pockets of his chinos, a wary determination hardening his face. "We have to talk," he said flatly.

Amber reeled, bumping her shoulder against the door frame, but she couldn't peel her gaze off him. He didn't look like a drowned rat now as he had that morning. He'd cut his hair, for the wedding presumably. It was just a matter of clipping and thinning it at the nape, but the effect was polished, stylish even. Suddenly she could imagine him not just on the deck of his boat or at his ease in a restaurant but in a boardroom or even a ballroom. He was bound to look absolutely devastating in a tuxedo. He looked marvelous now in freshly pressed chinos, buffed suede shoes and a dark brown polo shirt with the tail tucked behind a braided leather belt. She gulped and felt Walt at her back.

"How'd you get in here?" Walt demanded, shoving past her in the doorway.

Reece didn't take his eyes from Amber's face as he answered. "Linda gave me her key."

Walt muttered something under his breath, but Amber didn't bother listening. Reece was right. They did need to talk, clear the air. End it. Perhaps. She shook her head, frightened by her own ambiguity. She realized suddenly that in her heart she hadn't ended it at all. Not yet. Walt seemed to take her silence for repudiation.

"Get out," he said to Reece.

"No," Reece replied succinctly.

Walt started forward, but Amber raised a hand to stay him. Looking at Reece, she asked, "Where is Linda now?"

He softened considerably, his gaze overflowing with entreaty. "With Brit."

Amber nodded. She wouldn't have left the girl on her own just now, either. Linda had been vocal and adamant about her support for Reece, so it was no surprise that she would consent to help him in this. Whether or not this was something to be angry about, Amber would consider later. Meanwhile, she folded her arms and said evenly, "Let's get it over with. Say whatever you think you have to." She told herself that she was not encouraging him, that she just wanted to get the unpleasantness out of the way as quickly as possible.

He took his hands from his pockets and cracked the knuckles of the right with one powerful grip of the left. It was the first time she had seen him display a nervous mannerism. "First of all," he began, "just to set the record straight, I did come here and look you up at your father's behest."

Walt made a disgusted sound and slammed the door. "Tell us something we don't know."

A muscle ticked in the hollow of Reece's jaw, but he otherwise ignored Walt. "I make no apologies for that," he said to Amber. "A father has a right to be concerned about his daughter. I do apologize for not telling you the truth the very moment I realized how unfounded Rob's concerns about you are."

She lifted an eyebrow. "He warned you not to tell me he'd sent you, right?"

"Yes. He said you wouldn't talk to me if I did, and he was right about that much. But not about the rest."

She ignored the first part. It was true, so she wouldn't argue the point. The implications of the second seemed more important anyway. "Let me guess what he had to say about his only daughter. I'm an undisciplined, ungrateful, irresponsible child without the first notion how to get on in the world because I won't do exactly what he tells me to. Is that about it?"

"That pretty much sums it up," Reece agreed bluntly, surprising her for the first time. "The only thing I would add is that he truly does love you. He just doesn't seem to know how to do that without trying to control your every move."

"And how did you come to that conclusion?" she asked warily.

"I went to see him again while I was in Texas."

"To report, no doubt," she snapped, stung by the news.

"To tell him that I intended—intend—to marry you," he said firmly.

She blinked. It took a moment for that statement to settle in her brain. When it did, her heart began to pound. She turned away, saying lightly, "That must have been quite a conversation."

"Well, nobody's nose got busted, but it was a close thing," he muttered.

Amber stared at her hands. "What did he say?"

"What you'd expect, that you're too immature to know your own mind, that I've taken advantage of you, other things I'd just as soon forget. He made some stupid threats he couldn't possibly follow through, and then he took a swing at me. Your mom stepped in just as I was about to return the favor—very sensible of me, I know. Then I told him that you were absolutely right to take yourself as far away from him as you could get and that he would be welcome in our home only when and if he could treat you with the respect you deserve. Before I left, I also pointed out that his attitude would cut not only you from his life but our children as well.''

Children. Amber whirled around, galvanized by the concept. Their children. For a moment she couldn't breathe. Silence ensued, until Walt spoke.

''I bet the old man hit the roof over that!'' He tried to sound scathing, dismissive, and managed only to seem worried.

One corner of Reece's mouth quirked up. ''Actually,'' he said, never taking his eyes from Amber, ''Rob looked just about like Amber does now.'' She turned away again, aware that he'd read too much on her face. The next moment, he walked across the floor to stand directly behind her. ''If it's any comfort to you,'' he told her gently, ''you mom called me later to wish us well and say that your dad is showing signs of coming around. He apparently asked her if she thought he could be a better grandfather than he had been a father.''

Amber blinked back sudden tears. So there was hope that one day she might again be able to have a relationship with her father. She was glad, but it didn't address the matter of a relationship with Reece. How could she trust him again? No matter what her traitorous heart said, he had lied to her for weeks. She couldn't just forget that. And yet how could she face life without him? She blinked harder, determined not to cry, and felt his hands hovering about her upper arms. Part of her screamed out for him to touch her; part of her couldn't bear it. Walt inserted himself again.

''All right,'' he said, trying to sound commanding, ''you've had your say, now Amber needs some space.''

"Don't tell me what Amber needs," Reece snapped. "This isn't about what Amber needs. This is about you hoping she'll turn to you if I'm out of the picture."

"Hey! At least I didn't lie to her," Walt retorted. "I didn't pretend to be interested in her for myself when it was only her old man calling the shots."

"I never pretended," Reece said quietly. Then he seized Amber by the upper arms and turned her to face him. "You know that you'd never have given me the time of day if I'd told you about my connection with your father. As it was, getting you to talk to me was like pulling teeth, which was fine. I respect your caution."

"Don't listen, Amber," Walt warned. "You can't believe nothing he says."

"By the time I figured out the reality of the situation with your father," Reece went on doggedly, holding her gaze with his, "it was too late. I was falling in love with you. I didn't know what to do. I kept telling myself that the right time for the truth would come, and it did. But then everything went haywire. Brittany showed up, and I had to help her deal and take her back to Houston."

"You could have told me before you left," she accused.

"I could have, yes. I could have told you how very much I love you and then confessed everything—in the maybe five minutes of privacy we managed together before I had to leave for Texas. Would you have done it that way?"

She couldn't answer that, she was so confused. "I don't know."

"I wanted to set a stage for it, do something wildly romantic and unique. I bought an engagement ring in Houston, so you'd know that what I feel for you, what I want for us, has nothing to do with why I came here initially. I figured that I would fully discharge any duty I might have had to your father and maybe even bring back his blessing for you. That I wasn't able to do, regretfully, but I did try."

Amber sighed, more swayed than she wanted to admit. It must have shown, for suddenly Walt stomped his foot, proclaiming, "You can't listen to him!"

"It's not up to you!" Reece pointed out roughly, scowling at the other man.

"That's right. It's up to Amber, and she doesn't need you. She doesn't even want you. Just go back to wherever you came from and leave us alone!"

"I'm not going anywhere," Reece proclaimed, turning fully to face Walt, "unless Amber goes with me."

"That'll never happen!" Walt sneered, emboldened, Amber knew, by her silence. It was time to speak up.

"Actually I think we need to go someplace private and talk," she said softly.

They both looked at her. "Amber," Reece began, but Walt didn't let him finish.

"You don't mean that," he exclaimed, shouldering Reece aside. "You don't need him. We don't need him mucking everything up again!"

"There is no *we*, Walt," she said firmly.

Reece reached down for her hand then and, for the moment, she let him have it. Walt looked as though she'd hit him, and she regretted that. She should have faced up to this problem a long time ago. She should have told him the…truth. The truth. How easy it had been to live this particular lie, to pretend that she didn't know how he felt about her, to avoid the subject and the confrontation. And why hadn't she set him straight? Because it would have meant risking their friendship, of course, making her life uncomfortable, walking everywhere, living with his disappointment. Maybe she wasn't so different from Reece after all. She covered her mouth with her hand.

"I haven't ever lied to you," Walt muttered angrily.

"No, you haven't," she admitted, dropping her hand, "but I have lied to you in a way, because I never said outright what I've always known. I value your friendship, Walt, more than I can tell you, but I can never feel anything else for you. I can never love you like...you want me to."

Reece squeezed her hand, but she ignored him, her attention reserved for her dear friend. Poor Walt's face took on a forlorn look. He bowed his head. "If you'd just give me a chance," he whispered, but she shook her head.

"It wouldn't matter," she told him gently. "Walt, you're perfectly happy here on this island, living the easy, unhurried, tropical lifestyle. I'm not."

"I could try to—"

"That would be foolish and unfair," she interrupted. "You need someone who shares your fondness for this life, someone happy with just you, just as you are. That's not me. That could never be me."

Walt closed his eyes and swallowed. "You're going to take him back," he accused.

Was she? She wasn't sure yet. She shook free of Reece's hand and said, "We're just going to talk."

"That's all I ask," Reece said quickly. "Come out to the boat. Brittany will give us some space. I'll make dinner, and we'll talk about it. We'll decide together where we want to go from here."

She bit her lip. "And if I can't forgive you, because I'm not sure I can, you know?"

Something flitted across his face. Pain? Regret? Panic? "Just come with me tonight," he pleaded hoarsely, "and after we've said it all, if you want me to walk out of your life and never come back again, I'll...I'll do my best," he finally finished.

"Your best," she said skeptically. "What does that mean?"

He put both fists to his head. ''It means I won't lie to you and say that I'll disappear and never try to win you back because I'm not sure I can do that.'' He dropped his hands, gasping as if the words required great effort. ''But if it's what you want, I'll try.''

It was the right answer, the perfect answer, because she didn't want him to give up, not just yet. She wanted...she wanted to be able to trust him again, to love him and be loved by him. She just didn't know for sure that it was possible, but there was only one way to find out.

''All right.''

His relief was palpable. ''Thank you. Thank you.''

''Walt,'' she said, addressing the man standing slump-shouldered in the middle of the floor, one hand resting on the back of his neck. He slid a look sideways at her. ''We could use a lift,'' she said hopefully. For a moment, she thought he would refuse, but then he nodded resignedly.

''If it's what you want,'' he said.

She smiled wanly. ''I think it's the right thing to do.''

''You won't be sorry,'' Reece promised, ushering her toward the door as if afraid she'd change her mind. For good measure, he looked at the other man and said, ''Thank you, Walt. Linda will need a ride home, too.''

Walt grumbled something ungracious, but he followed them out the door and down the steps to the taxi. Reece opened the back door for Amber, and she got in, sliding all the way over to put some space between them. He seemed to respect that, but his hand rested on the seat between them, an open invitation. It required a great strength of will not to slip her own into it, but she managed to turn her face to the window and keep it there, her hands folded in her lap until they reached the dock.

Reece was grateful beyond words for this chance, but he knew, too, that everything, his entire future, hung in the balance. Every word, every action must be weighed carefully. He was determined to behave calmly, not to pressure her, not to make a scene, no matter that panic lurked beneath the confident surface he strove to present. Walt brought the taxi to a halt at the curb as close to the ice-cream stand as possible. He then quickly hopped out of the car to open Amber's door for her. She slipped out and looked around, anything, Reece suspected, to avoid him. Brittany leaped up from a nearby bench and waved enthusiastically. Linda was more subdued. Obviously she was worried about how Amber might perceive her actions. He hoped, for Linda's sake, that Amber wouldn't hold them against her. Amber hurried in that direction, but Reece held back. If necessary, he'd plead Linda's case to Amber later. Right now, he could do the girl more good by speaking to Walt.

He walked around the taxi to address the man, but Walt beat him to it. "You better not be yanking her chain," he growled, sticking his nose in Reece's face. Reece tamped down his irritation, reasoning that Walt's doubt and disdain were at least partially earned.

"I mean every word I've said," he told Walt firmly. "I love her, and I intend to marry her."

"If she'll have you."

"Well, we know she won't be having you, don't we?" Reece snapped.

Walt's face crumpled, and Reece immediately regretted the snide words. "Listen," he said earnestly, glancing in Amber's direction. She was hugging Brittany, a good sign, he hoped. Linda was smiling, so maybe that situation was going to work out well, too. "I know you're disappointed," Reece went on, "but Amber was never the woman for you."

"So you say," Walt sneered, "and we both know why."

Reece didn't bother denying it. Instead, he said, "Why don't you look around you? You've been spending all this time mooning over Amber, and someone else has been doing everything in her power to get your attention."

Walt frowned suspiciously. "What are you talking about?"

Reece nodded toward the tall, thin young woman standing next to Amber. "It's painfully obvious that Linda is crazy about you."

Walt's mouth fell open. "That's absurd! All we do is fight. She's constantly criticizing me for..."

"Chasing after Amber," Reece finished for him. "Now that ought to tell you something—unless you're not as smart as I think you are." He walked away, leaving it at that, but he could tell the other man was seriously considering what he'd said. He turned his attention to Amber. God, she was beautiful. He ached just looking at her and prayed that he'd find the words to make her forgive him.

He joined them in front of the ice cream stand, thanked Linda for all her help and slipped an arm around Brittany's shoulders. She was wringing her hands, but Amber felt incapable of reassuring the girl.

"I, um, thought I'd make chicken and mushroom tacos," he announced cheerfully after Linda had gone off with a subdued but thoughtful Walt.

Brittany said, "Yum," but Amber was dubious, and it obviously showed.

"Trust me," he quipped, adding cheekily, "at least with dinner." She gave him a look meant to peel paint. "Sorry," he muttered, carefully herding them toward the boardwalk.

The tense silence proved to be more than Brittany could bear. They hadn't even reached the skiff before she launched into a chatty description of her mother's wedding, a very elegant, dignified affair, apparently. Amber tried to appear interested and to make appropriate noises at all the right places, but in truth, she felt oddly removed from everything and everyone around her.

Once they reached the boat, Reece made dinner while Brittany chattered on and on and Amber watched the sunset in silence on the aft deck. Rather than inviting her inside to eat, Reece set up a table in the pilothouse and carried the food out to Amber and Brittany.

The chicken and mushroom tacos turned out to be quite tasty, but Amber couldn't really enjoy them. Some part of her was waiting, wondering, worrying. Could they really go on from here? Reece didn't seem to have much appetite, either. When he set aside his half-full plate, Brittany quickly grabbed it up along with Amber's and her own and carried them all below, insisting that she would clean up. She turned on music in the salon so they'd know she couldn't hear anything they were saying.

Unfortunately, they weren't saying much. They moved down onto the aft deck, Amber staring out across the harbor as night gathered, Reece staring at her. The silence stretched and stretched and stretched until, oddly enough, it began to feel comfortable. Finally, she turned to face him, and a question she hadn't even known she was going to ask tumbled out of her mouth. "Would you have made love to me that night?"

He slid his hands into his pockets and said, "Yes. If you had allowed it. Would you have?"

She looked down at her lap, wanting to lie to him, to herself. She didn't. "Yes."

"I'm glad we were interrupted then," he said softly.

She lifted her head and pinned him with a steady gaze. "Why?"

"Because," he said tenderly, "when I make love to

you, *every time* I make love to you for the rest of our lives, I want nothing between us but truth.''

Something fluttered inside her chest. ''It's a little late for that, isn't it?''

''No. It would have been if I'd made love to you that night, but now we have a chance to make it right between us and keep it that way.''

''Do you really think we can?'' she asked, a tingling in her chest making her short of breath. It was as if her heart had gone to sleep and was waking up again, like a foot or hand from which the circulation had been cut off.

He leaned forward, his elbows braced against his knees, hands clasped. ''I have to,'' he said earnestly. ''There are no other options for me. You fill up every empty space in me, Amber, and make me whole. With you I have a future, and without you I don't.''

She just sat there looking at him, until tears welled in her eyes. He reached out even as he stood, pulling her up and into his arms. She laid her cheek against his chest and closed her eyes, too weary and too much in love to fight her desires any longer. ''If you ever lie to me again,'' she began.

''I won't!'' he vowed. ''As God is my witness. I'm so sorry, honey. I should have told you the truth as soon as I realized that I was falling in love with you, but I was just so busy being happy and so afraid you would send me away. I'm not making excuses, really I'm not, but when we're together, you just knock every other thought right out of my head. You overwhelm me. What I feel for you is so strong it still amazes me.''

''I feel the same way,'' she admitted. ''That's why it hurt so badly to find out you'd lied to me.''

''Does that mean you'll forgive me and marry me?'' he asked desperately, cupping her face with his hands and tilting it up.

She grinned, feeling lighter and lighter by the second. "Can I just marry you now and leave the forgiveness for later?"

His eyes plumbed hers for a long moment, then a smile sliced open his face. "You're enjoying this, aren't you, me pouring out my heart at your feet?"

"Maybe," she answered coquettishly.

"Then let me do a proper job of it," he said solemnly. "I love you more than I can even begin to tell you. When I'm with you, the whole world is right, and when I'm not, nothing is. I look at you and see every dream I had at twenty-four and my only chance to actually make them come true. I'd given them up, you know, years ago, a wife who actually likes me, my best friend and lover, a houseful of happy kids."

Children again. Her heart flopped right over like a dog wanting a belly scratch. "How big a house?" she asked drolly.

He laughed. "That's strictly up to you, sweetheart. It's all up to you. My life begins or ends at thirty-eight, and it's strictly up to you which it is. If you love me enough to get past this and marry me, then it's perfect. If not..." He shook his head. "I can't even think about it."

She slipped her arms around his waist and leaned heavily into him. "Well, then, since I feel the very same way, I guess I'd better marry you."

He put his head back and gulped air. When he lowered his head again, tears slipped from his eyes. "Thank you! You won't regret it, I swear." He hugged her so tightly that she thought her ribs might crack.

"I know." She wiped his eyes with her fingertips, first one, then the other. He covered her mouth with his, the kiss so evocative and poignant that it warmed her inside and out. Her every doubt dissolved.

Something hissed insistently until they pulled apart to

turn toward the sound. Brittany grinned down at them from the pilothouse. Then she lifted her hand and pointed to her third finger.

"Oh!" Reece jammed his hand into his pants pocket and yanked it out again. "I forgot all about the ring!" He opened his fist, and Amber gasped. Platinum and a diamond weighing at least two karats. "If you don't like it, we can take it back," he said worriedly. "I want you to be completely happy, so don't worry about hurting my feelings."

Amber could only laugh. "It's beautiful!"

"Put it on! Put it on!" Brittany crowed. His hands were trembling as badly as Amber's as he slipped the ring onto her finger. "Okay, okay," Brittany exclaimed as they kissed again. She leapt down to the aft deck and said, "Wedding. When? Where?"

Reece looked at Amber. "My brother said we could have it at his place in Galveston with about a week's notice."

"You told your brother about me?"

"Honey, I told everyone who'd stand still about you," he confessed happily.

She felt such joy that she thought she just might burst with it. "Can we be in Galveston in a week?"

"Absolutely."

"I'll need a dress."

"We'll go shopping in Houston."

"Where are we going to live?" she asked, her mind working furiously.

"Anywhere you want. Literally."

She couldn't believe this. "Anywhere?"

"Anywhere in the world. In case I didn't mention it before, the business brought top dollar. We have enough money to last several lifetimes. In fact, I've been thinking about what you said about wanting to expose underprivileged children to theater, and I think we ought to create a facility just for that purpose, or maybe several facilities, wherever they're needed, with state-of-the-art equipment and—"

She threw her arms around his neck and pressed her mouth to his, overwhelmed by such loving generosity. He locked his arms around her and tilted his head, deepening the kiss. Amber forgot everything else, utterly mesmerized by the passion he so easily aroused in her—until Brittany huffed and exclaimed petulantly, "Boy, don't you guys ever come up for air?"

They broke apart, laughing, and Amber turned within the circle of Reece's arms to look at the girl apologetically. Brittany stood there, twisting her hands together, looking a little worried and left out. Suddenly Amber knew that she couldn't take Reece from his daughter, not for any reason. Besides, she wanted to go home, at least to Texas. "Houston," she announced firmly. "We'll definitely live in Houston."

Brittany suddenly rushed forward, throwing her arms around both of them, making a human sandwich of Amber, who hugged her close. The future had never looked so bright or so full of promise and love as it did through her happy tears. And forgiveness had never come so easily.

* * * * *

*Look for more unforgettable
love stories from beloved
author Arlene James
later in 2001.*

#1 *New York Times* bestselling author

NORA ROBERTS

brings you more of the loyal and loving,
tempestuous and tantalizing Stanislaski family.

Coming in February 2001

The Stanislaski Sisters

Natasha and Rachel

Though raised in the Old World traditions of their
family, fiery Natasha Stanislaski and cool, classy
Rachel Stanislaski are ready for a *new* world of love....

*And also available in February 2001 from
Silhouette Special Edition, the newest book in the
heartwarming Stanislaski saga*

CONSIDERING KATE

Natasha and Spencer Kimball's daughter Kate turns her
back on old dreams and returns to her hometown, where
she finds the *man* of her dreams.

Available at your favorite retail outlet.

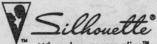

Where love comes alive™

Don't miss the reprisal of
Silhouette Romance's popular miniseries

When King Michael of Edenbourg goes missing,

Royally Wed

The Stanbury Crown

his devoted family and loyal subjects make it their mission to bring him home safely!

Their search begins March 2001 and continues through June 2001.

On sale March 2001: **THE EXPECTANT PRINCESS**
by bestselling author **Stella Bagwell** (SR #1504)

On sale April 2001: **THE BLACKSHEEP PRINCE'S BRIDE**
by rising star **Martha Shields** (SR #1510)

On sale May 2001: **CODE NAME: PRINCE**
by popular author **Valerie Parv** (SR #1516)

On sale June 2001: **AN OFFICER AND A PRINCESS**
by award-winning author **Carla Cassidy** (SR #1522)

Available at your favorite retail outlet.

Silhouette®

Where love comes alive™

Visit Silhouette at www.eHarlequin.com

SRWW3

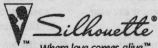

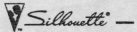

where love comes alive—online...

your romantic
books

♥ Shop online! Visit Shop eHarlequin and discover a wide selection of new releases and classic favorites at great discounted prices.

♥ Read our daily and weekly Internet exclusive serials, and participate in our interactive novel in the reading room.

♥ Ever dreamed of being a writer? Enter your chapter for a chance to become a featured author in our Writing Round Robin novel.

• • • • • •

your romantic
life

♥ Check out our feature articles on dating, flirting and other important romance topics and get your daily love dose with tips on how to keep the romance alive every day.

• • • • • • •

your
community

♥ Have a Heart-to-Heart with other members about the latest books and meet your favorite authors.

♥ Discuss your romantic dilemma in the Tales from the Heart message board.

your romantic
escapes

♥ Learn what the stars have in store for you with our daily Passionscopes and weekly Erotiscopes.

♥ Get the latest scoop on your favorite royals in Royal Romance.

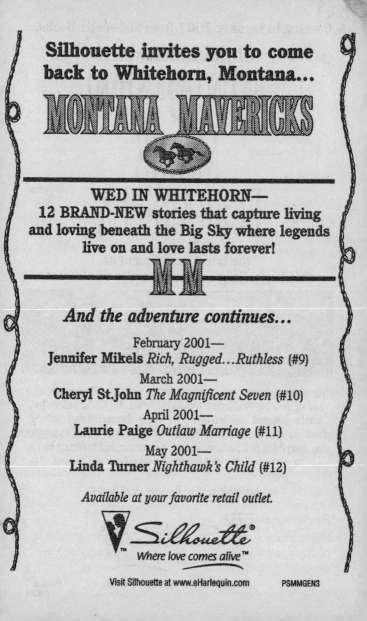